TRAIN OF
CONSEQUENCES

A Novel

TRAIN OF CONSEQUENCES

A Novel

TOM JARVIS

iUniverse, Inc.
New York   Bloomington

Train of Consequences

iUniverse books may be ordered through booksellers or by contacting:

iUniverse
1663 Liberty Drive
Bloomington, IN 47403
www.iuniverse.com
1-800-Authors (1-800-288-4677)

ISBN: 978-1-4502-6623-9 (pbk)
ISBN: 978-1-4502-6622-2 (cloth)
ISBN: 978-1-4502-6624-6 (ebk)

Library of Congress Control Number: 2010915437

Printed in the United States of America

iUniverse rev. date: 10/28/2010

Grateful acknowledgment is made for permission to reprint
excerpts from the following Metallica songs:

"Fixxxer" written by James Hetfield, Lars Ulrich, and Kirk Hammett.
Lyrics reprinted with permission of Creeping Death Music © 1997

"Dyers Eve" written by James Hetfield, Lars Ulrich, and Kirk Hammett.
Lyrics reprinted with permission of Creeping Death Music © 1988

This is for my first reader:
Tanja
My love, my life, always.
Without your support and encouragement,
this book would not exist.

Tell me, can you heal what father's done?
Or cut this rope and let us run?
Just when all seems fine and I'm pain free,
You jab another pin, jab another pin in me ...

— "Fixxxer" by Metallica

A brother is a friend God gave you;
A friend is a brother your heart chose for you.

— Ancient Proverb

Of all the thirty-six alternatives, running away is best.

— Chinese Proverb

PART ONE
MAN OF SORROWS

Chapter 1
CIGARETTES IN A MOTEL

October 2008

Waking from another one of those horrible dreams, I looked around the dark and unfamiliar room. For a moment, I forgot where I was, but the neon vacancy light reflecting off the wall quickly reminded me that I was in a musty motel outside Overture, New Hampshire. I glanced over at the faded green digital numbers on the nightstand clock. 3:23 AM. After I sat up in the bed, I looked out the motel room's window while I reached for a cigarette from my pack.

An autumn mist blanketed the ground outside under the trees. Illuminated from a streetlamp, I could see the reds, oranges, and yellows of the changing leaves that marked New England's main attraction in the fall. People from all over the globe came here to "leaf peep." Because I had grown up in New Hampshire, however, the leaves didn't impress me that much. I didn't come back here to see the foliage anyway.

I came home to visit my childhood friend, Richie Kemp.

A chill ran through me as I thought of my old friend. I slid my hand down the side of my stubbly face, the details of my bad dream fading like the night outside. Since I had turned thirty about three months back, I had endured recurring dreams about Richie and the terrible events of seventeen years ago. I began seeing a therapist about them at the urging of my girlfriend back in Cleveland. The therapist recommended this trip to my childhood hometown but only after I had told her about the "thirty-year caucus" agreement between Richie and me.

She explained that seeing Richie in my dreams—and my bad dreams in general—were some of the latent effects of post-traumatic stress disorder because of what had happened. During our most recent session, she said that I had never obtained "closure" to my friendship with Richie and that I still harbored unwarranted feelings of guilt and shame about how our relationship had ended. She suggested that a confrontation in this case would help, that if I honored the "thirty-year caucus" with Richie, I would gain closure and be able to start a new chapter in my life. Sounded like quite a sales pitch.

Sometimes I thought my therapist was full of shit.

Nevertheless, I bought into it. If anything, it was an excuse to get out of Cleveland and away from my girlfriend for a while. We'd begun to have "problems" because of my "fear of intimacy," which was probably the real reason that she wanted me to see a therapist in the first place. But maybe the therapist was right. Maybe visiting Richie would be the perfect opportunity to clear my conscience and move on with my life. I felt a little silly about the whole situation, really. I knew that Richie would remember our agreement, that if we were to ever lose touch, we would meet again when we turned thirty, but those were the words of two kids, not a binding contract.

Although I was only thirteen the last time I saw Richie, I could still clearly remember the details of his face and his infectious laugh. He had lively blue eyes, full cheeks, and a seemingly permanent smirk, which gave him a jovial and boyish appearance. His short mop of careless dark blond hair was so full of cowlicks that it looked messy no matter how many times he tried to fix it.

Soon after we became friends, he started calling me Shelly. It was annoying at first, because Shelly was a girl's name and I preferred Shelton. I was actually named after the jazz composer Shelton Brooks, whom my parents had loved during their happier days. But

Richie apparently had no appreciation for jazz, because he insisted on the nickname. He said that Shelly just sounded tougher.

"It's like those guys in the mafia movies, dude," Richie had said in his slight New York accent. "They didn't go by Anthony or James or Vincent. It was always Tony, Jimmy, or Vinnie, you know? Those were *tough* guys, and they had *tough*-sounding names."

I eventually gave up arguing with him about it. Richie had that way about him. When he was convinced of something, he made you a believer, too.

My older brother, John, died the year before Richie moved to New Hampshire. As a result, Richie just kind of slid into that role, even though he was only 364 days older than me. "Not a full year," Richie would say, "but still older and wiser." To which I would typically respond with a gem, "A wise *ass* maybe," hoping for a laugh of approval for my geniuslike wit.

Thinking about him now brought a mixture of nostalgic feelings to the surface. I stubbed my cigarette out in the tin ashtray on the motel's nightstand. *I really have to quit smoking,* I thought. As I looked around the room, I wondered if this motel had been here seventeen years ago. The faint odor of old cigarettes, moldy carpets, and stale urine certainly suggested that it had been around for a while, but I couldn't remember.

Overture was a very small town, but it exhibited a few city characteristics, such as a supermarket and a movie theater. We even had our own high school, which was more than you could say about most of the surrounding towns. Kids from Warner, Bradford, and Davisville all had to be bussed up to Kearsarge Regional High School in North Sutton. Consequently, the townsfolk borrowed from Reno, calling Overture "the biggest little town in New Hampshire."

The town itself sat almost directly in the center between Concord and the Vermont state border. There were two main sections of Overture, unofficially divided by the town hall. To the west of the town hall was the poorer section, dubbed by the townies as "Low Town." That was where the lumber mill was, sitting at the base of Mount Shea, and also where the gravel pit and the town dump were. To the east of the town hall lay the "upper crust" area, where the movers and the shakers lived. That side of town boasted the bank, the high school, and the post office.

If you were to look even closer at our little burg, you would also see that the two halves were broken down into even smaller sections. I lived on Shriner Way, two blocks from the high school, in the poorer part of the upper crust section. Luckily, my family had just enough money and status to stay out of Low Town. Richie wasn't so fortunate. He lived across town by the gravel pit on Calcutta Road, the poorest of the poor section. Or the lowest part of Low Town, so to speak.

I had just turned thirteen and was surviving the eighth grade when Richie moved here from New York in early 1991. His parents divorced after his father, Dino Gallo, was sentenced to thirty years in prison for crimes associated with the mafia. His mother then moved away from New York with Richie to escape the stigma.

I was a shy kid and had no friends to speak of when he moved to our town, especially because I was the kid whose brother died in that "awful wreck down by the shoe store." Death in the family had a way of making other people around you feel awkward and stay away. As if they were afraid they might catch it. Thinking back, I was most likely just as responsible as they were for my alienation, because I hated God and the world as a whole for taking my brother from me.

Richie was somewhat of an outcast as well, living in a single-parent home, forced to carry the baggage of his imprisoned father, and being the new kid from a big city. Because he had no friends either, we were naturally drawn to each other, and we became instant chums. We declared ourselves best friends in the rapid way that only children could.

We soon earned the reputation as the two goofballs of the school, often laughing wildly to ourselves when others didn't see what was so funny, coming up with silly shit like the thirty-year caucus, for instance. After school, we spent most of our free time together and developed a penchant for people mistaking us for brothers. We finished out that school year in style, raised hell all summer long, and then started our freshman year of high school beating our chests with our heads held high.

Despite the divorce and the move, Richie still seemed the happiest he'd ever been. Hell, that was when *I* was the happiest I'd been, too. A light was shining on us that year, for sure. But as life would have it, a dark cloud came along and brewed up a shit storm, and that dark cloud's name was Jim Kemp.

Jim was an auto mechanic at the Insty Lube, which was only three streets over from Richie's house. Richie's mother, Bianca, had taken her car in for service one day, and after about a week, Jim began servicing *her*, too. After a short courtship—if you could call nightly drunk sex a courtship—they married. Bianca took Jim's name and convinced him to adopt Richie as well, effectively ridding her and her son of the tarnished Gallo name once and for all. As such, Richie Gallo became Richie Kemp.

Soon after that, the abuse began, and my best friend was never the same.

As I gazed out of the motel room window into the dark New Hampshire woods, I lit another cigarette, knowing I probably wouldn't be able to get back to sleep. *It's going to be a long night,* I thought as I saw my haggard reflection in the window. My thoughts returned to the day when I first realized that something was very wrong with Richie. It was seventeen years ago on a crisp, fall day much like this one. Richie and I were skipping class ...

Chapter 2
PLANTING SEEDS

September 1991

The wind was a little strong that day, blowing through the streets of our quaint little town. The brittle and browning leaves on the ground would sometimes swirl around and float up only to fall back down dead again. I saw an attractive-looking woman wearing a bright yellow skirt, coming out of Christy's Market with a bag of groceries in one hand and modestly holding down her skirt with the other. She skittered toward her car like that, trying to keep the wind from exposing her panties to the world, and I found it rather amusing. So amusing that I didn't hear what Richie said to me. I was only faintly aware that he was talking to me.

"Shelly, are you listening to me?"

"Yeah, sorry," I said, turning my head to look at Richie. The wind had comically tousled his cowlicks, but he didn't seem to notice or care.

"Have you ever thought of running away?" He repeated.

"Running away?"

"Do I *stutter*?" He teased, trying to impersonate John Bender from *The Breakfast Club*. He was leaning against the brick wall of the church across the street from the high school, smoking a cigarette. The students called this area the "Backyard." This was the place to go, for some of us, to meet before school in the morning and to "smoke butts" when you were cutting class. The Backyard was virtually a hidden alleyway set between the windowless sides of an old church and an out-of-business day care. It was visible only from Christy's Market on one side of the alley and a vacant lot on the other.

Mr. Underhill, the owner of Christy's, never ratted any of us out for skipping or smoking, because we made up a large portion of his business. In fact, he provided a few accommodations for us, such as empty milk crates for seating purposes and a trash can that he emptied once a week. He also swept up our dead cigarette butts each night before he closed up the store. He made quite a chunk of money from us delinquents by turning a blind eye as long as we bought our cigarettes, sodas, and snacks there. This was about a year or two before the government began heavily cracking down on tobacco sales to minors. Likewise, Overture was surprisingly lax regarding truancy. Lucky for us.

"No, but you talk like you have a load of shit in your mouth," I said in response to Richie's stutter question.

"And you talk like you have a dick in yours."

"Fuck you."

"Seriously, dude," he said. "You can't tell me you've never thought about just packing up your shit and bailing."

I stuffed my hands in my pockets and shrugged, looking down at a cigarette butt on the ground. I had never thought about running away. Things were pretty crazy at my house, but even so, home was … *home.*

"Come on, man," he said. "The way you make it sound, your parents would be happier if you were gone. Maybe if you were out of the house, they wouldn't even get a divorce, you know? You could start living on your own."

"Living on my own?"

"Here we go again," he said. "I really must be stuttering."

"Shut up, dude. Where the hell would I go? What would I do? I mean, why are you asking me this stuff anyway?" I paused and then added, "Do *you* think about running away?"

Richie took a long drag off of his cigarette and absently moved his hand up to his ribs, wincing a little. Before he looked away, I thought I saw an expression of deep fear on his face. It scared me, that look. It seemed … helpless, even desperate. Then he took another drag, turned toward me with his trademark grin, and punched me in the arm.

"Come on, man. Do you always have to be so serious?"

"Hey, you're the one who brought it up," I said, rubbing my arm. *His stepfather must have been drunk again last night*, I thought. I had seen bruises on Richie before. He attempted to hide them, and he usually made up some lame excuse about what the bruises were from; however, I knew it was Jim. Richie was probably aware that I knew, but he obviously didn't want to talk about it. I tried to respect that and not ask any questions. I mostly just gleaned bits and pieces from the general things he told me. He once relayed how Jim would get so drunk sometimes that he would piss on the floor in the living room and then make Richie's mother clean it up. If she gave him any lip about it, he would backhand her.

Judging from the frequency and size of the bruises, it seemed like it was Richie who got the brunt of Jim's anger. The most disturbing detail that Richie had let slip one time was that he and his mother were particularly cautious of pissing Jim off on the days when he was wearing his steel-toed boots. The implications of that made me cringe.

I had met Jim only once. Richie often came over my house, but he never wanted me to go over to his. At first, he used the excuse that my house was closer to our school, but after a while, I realized that he just didn't want me over there. I assumed he was just too ashamed of his home.

Then, one time, I had pressed the matter, suggesting that we hang out at his house, because I didn't feel like being at mine. His face filled with panic, and he abruptly told me that I could *never* come over. I almost laughed until I realized that he was serious. When I asked him why, he said in a low, fearful tone that Jim got very angry if he and his mother had visitors. I wasn't sure if that meant Jim would be angry at *him* or at the visitor, but the sight of Richie's bruises made me not want to find out either way. And Richie's unwavering gaze told me that he didn't want to discuss it any further, so I dropped it.

But one school day, Richie stayed home sick, and our math teacher, Mr. Crawford, asked if there was anyone who could bring Richie's assignments to his house after school. Mr. Crawford had no sympathy for the sick and often assumed they were lying, so this was no surprise. As Richie's best and only friend, I automatically raised my hand before I realized what I was doing, and so I became the volunteer.

As I walked to Richie's house that day after school, my balls felt like they wanted to crawl up my ass and stay there. I wasn't sure why. I guess subconsciously I felt I was betraying Richie's wishes and expected him to be pissed off to see me on his doorstep. *But why should he be pissed off? Aren't I his best friend?* Remembering his chilly warning about Jim's dislike of visitors, however, made me want to turn back. Then again, I thought Richie could have been exaggerating. *So if he's exaggerating, then what's the big deal? He knows I don't care that his family is poor, so there shouldn't be anything to be ashamed of.* Those thoughts allowed me to pick my feet up off the ground and keep walking toward his house. When I rounded the corner from Blaine Street to Calcutta Road and saw house number twenty-two, however, an inexplicable wave of nausea gripped me. *What the hell is wrong with me?* I thought.

As I approached the house, I glanced around and counted four rusting cars up on cinderblocks strewn about the front yard, along with a snow mobile sporting a sun-faded "For Sale" sign on its cracked windshield. A shiny red IROC-Z sat parked in the driveway. The visible areas of the lawn were yellowed and even bare in some patches, and the cracked concrete walkway was decorated with assorted litter: a Budweiser bottle cap here, an empty and crumpled pack of Marlboro cigarettes there.

The house itself was in no better condition. Two of the windows were covered with black trash bags and masking tape, while the wood clapboard siding appeared to be rotting in some areas. Some of the shingles were missing from the roof, and those that remained were curled up at the edges like chocolate shavings. The entire structure seemed to have a sagging quality to it, leaning toward the left a little like a plant reaching toward the sun.

As I climbed the short set of stairs to the front door, I heard a man yelling inside. It was muffled, and though I couldn't understand the words, it sure didn't sound happy. *Must be Jim*, I thought. I raised my hand up to the door, hesitated for a moment, and then gingerly knocked. Closer to the door now, I could hear the voice from inside ask, "Who the hell is that?" The anger in his voice made me want to run away, but my feet felt like someone had poured cement around them.

The door opened, and a big man with a receding hairline and a salt-and-pepper handlebar mustache appeared. His green eyes were bloodshot, and his cheeks had a red tinge to them. The wrinkles around his eyes and his thick, black eyebrows formed what looked like a permanent scowl. Absurdly, I noticed that he had one hair sticking out of his mustache that was longer than all of the others. He towered over me, wearing a soiled white tank top, a pair of green Dockers with grease stains, and scuffed work boots.

"Who are you?" he asked. He was visibly drunk and smelled of booze, with disheveled hair and a slight sway. I backed up a step without thinking. He seemed to notice this and was pleased by it. A devious grin formed at the corners of his chapped lips, which made my legs almost buckle. I cleared my throat and managed to stammer out my words.

"I'm Shelton. I'm a friend of Richie's. Mr. Crawford asked me to bring him today's assignments, since he wasn't in school today"

"Well, come on in then," Jim said. He let out a rough chortle that sounded like he had ten razor blades in his throat. Then he turned and yelled up the stairs, "Richie, someone's here to see you."

I reluctantly stepped inside, and Jim stumbled over to a recliner in front of the television, practically falling into it. A green work shirt with a patch reading "Jimbo" was draped over the back of the recliner. I stared at the patch as I waited by the door, trying to avoid looking Jim in the face again, but I could feel his eyes burning into me. I risked a look and saw him staring at me, head swaying and open-mouthed, with a creepy gleam in his eye.

After what felt like an eternity, Richie finally crept down the stairs. The left side of his lower lip was swollen, and despite his noble attempt at hiding it, I could see that he had been crying. His face was pale and streaked with dirt. I had the sudden urge to reach out to him and hug him, but I resisted, because Jim was watching and Richie would probably punch me for that anyway. As he stepped down from the bottom stair, I couldn't help but notice him glance nervously at Jim.

"What are you doing here?" Richie asked, but his panicky tone suggested that he was more shocked and scared than he was angry.

"Mr. Crawford wanted me to give you your homework for today," I blurted, sounding more defensive than I meant to. "He doesn't believe you're sick, so he says you're still on the hook for the assignment."

"Yeah, Richie here is a real *sick puppy*," Jim said, letting out another throaty laugh. Richie looked over at Jim, and I saw something pass between them as their eyes met. It gave me the chills.

"Yeah, okay," Richie said. He absently took the papers from me and briskly motioned for me to go. "I'll see you tomorrow, dude."

As I turned to leave, Jim asked, "Why don't you stick around and hang out for a little bit? I'm sure Richie would love some company."

I looked back toward Richie and saw a pleading in his eyes. I shook my head and told Jim that I had to get home and couldn't stay. A visible wave of relief swept across Richie's face.

I left that day, hoping I would never again have to see that awful man.

Now, when I saw Richie holding his ribs, I immediately envisioned the unsettling image of him propped up on all fours and trying to pull himself up, and then Jim's work boot suddenly smashing into his side.

As I was about to say something to Richie on the subject of running away, we heard the sound of the school bell across the street signaling the end of the class in session. Richie quickly threw his cigarette down and stepped on it, telling me he couldn't be late to his next class. I stayed a moment longer and watched him go. That was when I noticed that Richie was slightly limping.

I turned back toward Christy's Market, hoping to catch a glimpse of that woman's skivvies, but she was long gone. Instead, there was an old man in plaid pants hobbling toward the store, scratching his ass. He was met by another old man leaving the store. They shook hands and began a conversation. The other man had no idea that the hand he just shook was previously knuckle-deep in hemorrhoids. That was enough for me. I stubbed out my cigarette and headed to class.

*   *   *

That day after school, I got home just in time to overhear yet another fight between my mother and father. Lucky me.

I stood in the foyer of the house for a moment, listening to them. From the sound of it, the argument was a continuation from that morning's barn burner. Since my brother died, each of their battles seemed to exceed the previous one by degrees of intensity. They both seemed to be taking out their guilt and regret on each other. Even if they were arguing about something minor like a wrinkled shirt or a misplaced sigh, the underlying argument was still there behind their words. It had begun with them blaming themselves for John's death, and before long, they pointed their fingers at each other. From there, it evolved into these furious feuds typically ending with one of them spouting off the big "D" word.

Most of the time, I felt invisible around them. The occasions when they actually did speak to me, they were cold and detached. I got the feeling that they resented me for being alive, that they maybe wished I had died instead of John. They never came out and said that, but the feeling was still there. Those feelings began even on the day that John had died.

The day it happened, I had been sitting in my room listening to music and reading along with the lyrics. I was waiting patiently for John to come home, so he could teach me how to play Stratego.

My father came into my room and turned my stereo off. I was just about to yell at him when I saw his face and realized something was terribly wrong. His eyes were wet and bloodshot, and he wore a sunken expression.

He sat down beside me, took a deep breath, and looked at me with despair. I began to feel scared, not even knowing why, and tears welled up in my eyes. I knew something horrible had happened. He told me that John had been in a terrible car accident. Understanding dawned on me, and I bawled, clutching my father.

"No, no, Dad … no. Not John … please."

My father nodded and closed his eyes as I continued to cry. After a moment, my father stood up and walked out of my room. He didn't look back or say anything else. I was astonished. I had just received the worst news of my life, and my father had walked out on me. I tried to understand it, to tell myself that he was grieving in his own way, but the damage had already been done.

I suddenly felt like I couldn't breathe. I sprang up off the bed and sprinted downstairs past my mother, who was weeping on the couch, and I threw open the front door. I ran out into the front yard and tripped over my own foot, crashing down into the snow. I didn't try to get up after that. I just lay there and cried. My brother was dead, and he wasn't coming back.

After a few minutes, it started snowing again, but I didn't care. I was frozen in grief. I stayed there in the snow, crying until I couldn't cry anymore. Neither of my parents came out to check on me or to bring me in from the cold. When I came back in the house later, I saw that my mother had fallen asleep on the couch and that my father was upstairs sleeping in their bed.

The next day, my mother served breakfast to us and sipped at her coffee, silently going through the motions. My father just stared at his plate through teary eyes. They barely even looked at me. It was almost like my presence just reminded them of the fact that they only had one son left. I wished there was something I could have done to fix things, to turn back time like in the *Superman* movie, but I couldn't even fly, let alone rotate the earth.

I hated seeing my parents in so much pain, too. Especially my father. Seeing him cry was devastating to me. He was my big bad dad. He wasn't supposed to cry. But that didn't excuse him and my mother for forgetting about me. They had lost John, but *I* had lost him, too. They seemed to have forgotten that. They were too wrapped up in their own grief to consider mine, and sometimes I hated them for that.

I couldn't understand why they had begun to treat each other so badly, either. I found it particularly mind-numbing. The floors of my house may as well have been made of eggshells as far as I was concerned. It seemed as though my parents were constantly on the lookout for the slightest reason to blow up at one another, and I was sometimes caught in the crossfire, searching for the nearest exit.

Back in what I call their "happier days," when I was younger and John was still alive, they would tell me things like, "Mommy and Daddy still love each other Shelton. We're just working out a difference of opinion," after a rare argument. John, whose bedroom was closer to theirs, told me one morning while he was poking my ribs, "I think they got over their differences last night if you know what I mean, Shel. Jesus Christ, I had to grab onto my bedposts and hold on for dear life, because the walls were shaking so much."

Back then, I could always count on John to make me laugh and feel like everything would be okay. But now John was dead. I was alone, and my parents didn't bother hiding their fights from me.

From the heating vent in my bedroom, I often overheard their discussions about separation turn into shouting matches about divorce and then further graduate to an all-out war about who got what when they were finally rid of each other. Their fights typically ended with a slam of the door, either by my mother going to their bedroom or by my father going outside to "cool off."

On some nights, they would have more productive discussions to "iron out the details." It was during one of those discussions that I first heard them use the word *custody.*

That was what they were "discussing" now. From the foyer, I could just picture my mother standing in the kitchen, probably cutting up some celery or an onion and my father most likely sitting on the couch, rolling his eyes, and trying to watch television.

"Naturally, he should stay with me," my mom said. "I'm his mother."

"The kid needs his father. If he stays with you, he might become a momma's boy or something."

"He can't live in an unstable environment, Doug."

"What do you mean by that?"

"I mean that once you're back on the market, you'll probably have strange women at your house all the time. I don't want my son exposed to that."

"Jesus Christ, Sarah. You don't—"

"Besides, you haven't even figured out what you want to do with your own life, let alone be responsible for *another* life."

"That's not fair, and you *know* it," my father said. "I wouldn't be exposing him to anything."

"Well, I don't want to take that chance. He's—"

"You know I'm a responsible father. You're being ridiculous."

"I'm not—"

"How could you even insinuate otherwise? He'll be fine with me."

"But—"

"*You're* the one who wants to go back to school. How are *you* going to have time for him?"

"*Goddamn it*," my mother yelled. "*He's my son, and I will find the time.*" She was typically the first to raise her voice. Most of the time, my father would be calm and try to keep things low-key, but my mother had a tendency to fly off the handle. My father would then try to remain calm for a while, but he would eventually lose his cool as well. At least he wasn't physical, though. He never laid a hand on my mother or me, and I was thankful for that.

I knew exactly where this conversation was headed, and I didn't want to listen to another word of it. Soon, they would both be yelling at the top of their lungs. I headed upstairs to my room and turned on the stereo. I popped in a Metallica CD, skipped to track nine, and turned up the volume to drown out my parents' bickering. I let my thoughts wander while James Hetfield's powerful voice drifted out of the speakers, asking, "Dear mother, dear father, what is this hell you have put me through?"

This was my perfect escape song. I listened to it whenever my parents were squabbling over me like a possession. I hated to hear their hurtful words toward each other. One time, I heard my mother tell my father during a custody discussion that he "didn't even want another baby in the first place". My father had denied it, saying that she was just grasping at straws, but the words continued to linger in my mind.

Is that possible? I asked myself. *Would my parents still be happy if I had never been born? Perhaps if John were an only child, God wouldn't have taken him away from them?*

As the mighty Hetfield shouted angrily through my stereo, I was reminded of Richie. It was obvious that his stepfather was hurting him. Richie himself had all but admitted to it, but it seemed like there was something more. Richie had always seemed so strong to me. I always thought of him as someone who would laugh in the face of the devil, unlike me, who was dreadfully afraid of any type of confrontation. I just couldn't figure out why he had briefly looked so helpless and desperate that morning in the Backyard.

I wished there was something I could do to help him. I thought about telling my parents, but I doubted they would listen to me. They probably wouldn't even care. They hardly even noticed when Richie was over at our house anyway. I couldn't call the police or the school, either. I was afraid that if I did, the backlash would be severe. Jim could even *cripple* Richie. Besides, I thought it would have been a betrayal to go behind Richie's back like that.

I was jolted out of my thoughts when the fucking CD began to skip. I ejected the disc and flipped on the radio. It was tuned to WGIR Rock 101, and they were playing an '80s rock block. The song "Runaway" was almost finished. As Jon Bon Jovi's extraordinary voice wafted up to my ears, I began to think of what Richie had talked about earlier in the Backyard.

What's going on in that head of yours, Richie? Were you serious about running away? I thought. *I'll have to talk to him more about it tomorrow at school. Maybe he was blowing smoke up my ass.* Just as the Bon Jovi song was fading out and being replaced by the signature riff of "Bark at the Moon" by Ozzy Osbourne, I heard the slam of the front door.

The fight was over for now.

* * *

The next morning, I arrived at the Backyard before Richie, so I sat down on an empty milk crate to wait for him. I contemplated whether or not I wanted to walk over to Christy's to buy a Coke. *Screw it*, I thought. I didn't feel like getting up. I wasn't really thirsty anyway. I just wanted something to wash back the taste of the stale cigarette I was smoking. No one else had arrived yet in the Backyard this morning either, so I wasn't able to bum a fresh one. *Oh well.*

The wind had died down a little over the course of the evening, but there was still a slight breeze. As I was zipping up my windbreaker, I spied a cat approaching from the vacant lot side of the alleyway. He trotted toward me, meowing. If John were there, he might have something to make me laugh like, "I assume he is a he, because he looks like a he to me, although I did not open up his legs to see."

He was a tabby cat, dressed in gray and black stripes, with white paws. As he got closer, I observed that his chin and chest bore white fur as well.

The tabby rubbed against my leg and raised his ass in the air, purring loudly. *What a cute cat*, I thought. As I reached down to pat him, I noticed that half of one of his ears was missing. It looked like someone had sliced the tip of it clean off. Poor thing. He seemed to be over it though, because he jumped up on my lap and looked me right in the eye, still purring. It may sound silly, but right then and there, I loved that cat. I didn't even know his name, but I somehow felt a deep connection with him all the same. With animals, it's just that simple, I guessed. There's no fakeness with them. When they look you in the eyes, it's sincerity all the way.

I wondered if he was a stray. He didn't have a collar, so it was hard to tell. He didn't look overly skinny and malnourished like some cats did when they lived on the streets. A strange thought entered my mind that he was searching for someone. I wasn't sure where the idea came from, but it just seemed right. Smiling, I ran my fingers through the soft fur on the sides of his face and scratched under his chin. He soaked it up like it was the best goddamned thing that had ever happened to him.

Suddenly, I felt a stinging compulsion to wrap my arms around him and take him home. I had never wanted a cat before, but he would keep me company. He would make me feel less alone while my parents were at it. I began to think it through. Where would I put him until I got out of school? If I brought him home right now and left him there for the day, there was always a chance that one of my parents would get home early. My mother might chase it out with a broom. Even if I were to ask them for a cat, would my parents allow it? I didn't think so. *My mother would probably wrinkle her nose at him and tell me that strays carried diseases or something,* I thought. *My father might be more inclined to go door to door, searching for the owner.*

Just then, the cat turned away, jumped down from my lap, and loped off. I stood up to go after him and stopped when he halted and turned toward me. He looked me in the eyes again briefly, turned back, and soon disappeared from the alley and from my life. I sat back down, feeling defeated. A sort of emptiness washed over me. Then reality set in, and I felt absurd. *Just a cat. Don't be silly,* I told myself. *Even with a cat, you would still feel alone.*

Just as I had resigned myself to a catless existence, Richie came around the corner into the Backyard. I noticed that his limp seemed more pronounced today. I asked him about it this time, and he shrugged it off.

"You know it's the damnedest thing. I twisted my ankle getting out of the shower," he said.

When he told me, his eyes guiltily darted away. It was obvious he was lying. I wished that he would just come out and tell me. *Does he think I'm stupid?* I thought. *Or worse, does he think he can't trust me?*

"So anyways, what happened on the latest episode of *As the Stomach Turns*?" Richie asked. "How are things at the Cole residence?" He squatted down to sit on the crate next to me but then seemed to think better of it and stood back up again with a wince. He shot a look at me that seemed to imply that it wouldn't have been a good idea for me to comment on it, so I didn't.

"Same shit, different day," I answered. "Hey, speaking of episodes, did you watch *America's Funniest Home Videos* last night?"

"No, man. Bob Saget's way too corny. Personally, I think him and Vanilla Ice should come out of the closet together."

I laughed, trying to forget about Richie not being able to sit.

"I watched *Seinfeld*, though," he said. "It was so funny. Jerry and George went and got massages, and the one that George got was from a guy, so George started thinking that maybe he's gay 'cause *it moved* when the guy massaged his thigh."

"That's wicked funny," I said with a chuckle.

"And then when Jerry got *his* massage, the woman was talking about her kid, and for some reason, Jerry starts talking about some guy he heard about who was kidnapping kids. And she got all freaked out with Jerry! You gotta watch this show, man. It's so funny."

"Yeah, I want to watch it, but my dad hogs the TV."

"That sucks."

"Yeah, he pretty much only watches the funny videos or the news," I said. "And when he's not home, my mom is watching *Roseanne* or *MacGyver*."

Richie stuck out his tongue and mimed putting his finger down his throat. I didn't think that was fair, because I liked both shows and they were both very successful. But I just shrugged instead of arguing.

"I swear though, neither one of them is really watching the TV. It's like they're just looking at it, you know?"

"Yeah, I hear you," Richie said. "Jim usually *owns* our TV every night, but last night, he passed out early after—"

He stopped himself and looked down at the ground.

I waited quietly, hoping that if I didn't say anything, he would continue. I wanted him to talk to me if he needed to. I was his best friend, and he was keeping this stuff bottled up. He needed to stop pretending that Jim didn't hit him. He needed to talk to someone. He almost did, too. He looked up at me, his mouth poised slightly open and seemingly about to speak, almost as if he *needed* to speak.

But then he closed his mouth and looked down at the ground again. We sat in an uncomfortable silence for a few moments.

"Yeah right, you fag," I teased, trying to mitigate the uneasiness. "You probably wait until everyone goes to bed, and then you sit and jerk off while watching episodes of *90210*."

"Talk to the hand, dickhead," Richie responded in a feminine voice with a lisp. It sounded even funnier with his faint New York accent.

"Talk to the finger, 'cause you ain't worth the whole hand, fuck face."

"Ooooow! You hurt my feelings," Richie said mockingly, clutching his chest and mimicking a fit of sobs. And just like that, the awkwardness was gone. Richie seemed to have collected himself. But once the school bell rang, I couldn't help but see that he looked grateful. I also couldn't help but wonder what was happening to my friend. I had been so wrapped up in what was going on with my parents lately that I hadn't noticed the changes in him.

The physical injuries were easy enough to see, but it was the other stuff that I hadn't noticed. Like how pale his face looked and how he seemed distracted and apathetic, with something like anger boiling just beneath the surface. I also felt that same feeling from the previous day, a sort of desperation emanating from him. That worried me a lot. Apprehension gripped me as I followed him into the school.

I suddenly felt very afraid for my friend, recalling an old adage: desperate people do desperate things.

Chapter 3
WUZZY

Richie and I met again for lunch that day as we did every day, sitting down at our usual table in the cafeteria. Richie put his tray down, and we commenced our daily food trade. Today, it was my french fries for his brownie. Yesterday, it was my corn bread for his green beans. Unbeknownst to me at the time, we wouldn't be trading food tomorrow.

"Do you think she uses teeth like that when she's blowing Mr. Camden?" Richie asked.

I followed his gaze to the other table and saw Tiffany Meier leaning over her tray, taking a bite out of a hotdog. I giggled quietly and then felt guilty. Tiffany was *rumored* to be an easy girl at our school, our gym teacher, Mr. Camden, being the latest of her supposed exploits. Of course, rumors were like contagious diseases in high school. Easy to catch, and they spread quickly.

Richie and I had recently found out the truth, though. The vindictive scuttlebutt all generated from the same source, a jock named Jason Labonville. He had accosted Tiffany at the beginning of the school year on her way home. She thwarted his advances, and his ego was bruised, so of course, he felt he had to do *something*. He couldn't have people thinking that he was undesirable to anyone.

23

Despite the fact that we had learned the truth behind the rumors, Richie still spoke as if he believed them as a dig toward me. He did so because I had a *major* crush on Tiffany.

She was like a precious gem to me, seemingly unattainable yet irresistible. She had long and wavy strawberry blonde hair that stopped at the swell of her budding breasts, with freckles dotting her nose and cheeks. Her delicate eyes were the color of emeralds, and her nose had the cutest little upward curve at the tip that looked as if a tiny skier could jump right off the end of it. Most of all, I was mesmerized by her exquisite lips. They had a slight pout to them that created an intriguing mystery I was eager to investigate.

I had two classes with her, and I always looked forward to them. Sometimes, I would summon the courage to speak with her, but it was little more than small talk.

"Come on, man," I said. "Cut it out. She's not blowing anybody."

"Maybe so, but I bet you wish she was blowing you."

"Well," I said, feeling hot blood rush to my cheeks.

"Why don't you just bite the bullet, dude?"

"Bite the bullet?"

Richie rolled his eyes and sighed loudly in an exaggerated display of irritation, and I smiled in spite of myself.

"Ask her out, dipshit," Richie said. "Go over there and whip it out for her and see if she latches on."

"You're vulgar," I said.

"And you're queer."

"It takes one to know one."

"Nice comeback, nancy," he said. "Let me ask you something. Does your train of thought have a caboose?"

I guffawed with a snort. As I put my hand up to my mouth to stifle it, I noticed Tiffany looking over at me. She smiled brightly, sending pangs of heat through my body. I tried to play it cool and smiled back, probably looking like a bumbling idiot in the process. Her eyes dropped down and then eased back up slowly and flirtatiously. The bottom half of my body seemed to go numb, and my throat suddenly felt very dry. I grabbed my carton of milk and drank, only vaguely aware that Richie was looking at me with amusement.

"Did you ever hear of the man with two assholes?" he asked, grinning widely.

I belted out laughing and milk sprayed from my nose and mouth, making me choke and laugh at the same time. Seeing this made Richie howl, and he almost fell out of his chair, which of course, sent me into a second fit of uncontrollable laughter. He tried to say something that only came out as "wha—" and then erupted again.

I sobered a little when I observed Tiffany's perplexed face. Our eyes met, and she managed to look amused and annoyed at the same time. I turned away, stung with embarrassment. Richie seemed to be collecting himself as well when someone spoke from behind him.

"Whatchoo bitches laughin' at?"

I looked up; already knowing to whom the voice belonged. His parents had named him Eddie, but everyone else just called him Wuzzy, short for his last name, Wuszelenski. He was what some would have called our school bully, but the students of Overture High considered him our school *terrorist*. He had been held back for two years already, making him the oldest student at Overture High. Consequently, he was also the biggest.

Wuzzy was a rap music aficionado and wore his colors proudly. He could typically be seen sporting a backward hat and loose clothing, which most of the teachers had given up trying to tell him not to wear, and he was the only student that had grown significant facial hair, fashioned into a goatee. Because he was a white person who talked and dressed black, some of the other kids dubbed him a "wigger" behind his back.

His reputation was furthered by tall tales, the biggest of which involved a kid named David Sweeney being sent to the hospital, almost dying, two years prior. David had pissed Wuzzy off in some way after school, probably by breathing his air or something, and foolishly attempted to flee. Wuzzy chased him across the football field, and when he caught up with him, he administered an "epic beat-down" to David for making him run for so long.

During the beating, David began to cough and wheeze, and

then he stopped moving. As soon as Wuzzy noticed, he fled the scene while a bystander ran to get help. All of the spectators were convinced that David was dead or dying as he was brought to the hospital in an ambulance. Once there, the doctor determined that David had suffered from anaphylaxis because of a severe allergic reaction to a bee sting. The bee must have stung David in midair during his flight from Wuzzy, and his reaction to it had unfolded during the brawl.

Somehow, two years after the incident, the bee was now left out of the story, most likely omitted intentionally by one of Wuzzy's crew or by Wuzzy himself, and it was told that Wuzzy beat David Sweeney so badly that he was carried away in an ambulance and almost died.

Wuzzy was proud of this story, as he was of his other similar achievements, and took a sick pride instilling fear in other students. His terror was sometimes directed at kids who looked at him wrong or who had the unfortunate luck of being in front of him in a line, but he mostly targeted freshmen like Richie and me. He particularly focused on Richie lately. There wasn't any apparent reason for this campaign; Richie had done nothing to instigate Wuzzy. Perhaps Wuzzy had seen a weakness in Richie. Most likely, Wuzzy had seen Richie's occasional black eye or fat lip and had determined him to be easy pickings.

"Hey, I'm talkin' to you, you little bitch," Wuzzy said.

Richie hadn't turned around yet. He continued to look at me sitting across from him. He looked scared, but he also looked … angry. I couldn't believe he had the balls to ignore Wuzzy like that. *No one* ignored Wuzzy. I felt terribly afraid for him for the second time that day. I didn't want him to end up like David Sweeney. I tried to urge him to cooperate, craning my neck forward and widening my eyes. But Richie stared forward unrelentingly and unblinking. I thought he had lost his mind.

"You'd better turn 'round if you know what's good for you, Kemp," Wuzzy said. He nudged Richie in the back with his knuckles, his two lackeys of the week looking on in disbelief.

"I'm not in the mood to deal with your bullshit, Wuzzy,"

Richie said. I heard a collective gasp from the other students in the immediate vicinity. I even saw a couple of them pick up their trays and move to another table. I saw Richie's hands trembling, and I looked away quickly, not wanting Wuzzy or his lackeys to see what I was looking at. Richie told me later that he had wanted to shit his pants at that point.

Wuzzy stepped back, visibly stunned. "What did you say?"

"I said just leave us alone. Go find someone else."

From the corner of my eye, I noticed Tiffany and her friends looking at us with sympathy and fright. I scanned the room, looking for the closest teacher and not finding one.

"P-p-please, Wuzzy, he's just having a bad time today. H-he doesn't mean it," I stammered, pleading for my friend.

"You shut up, Cole. Dis is between me and Kemp here. Or mebbe you want summa dis?"

Wuzzy moved as if he was going to come over to my side of the table, and Richie sprang to his feet and stood in front of him. From where I was sitting, I couldn't see Richie's face, but something in it made Wuzzy take a step back, momentarily unsure of himself. Then, just as quickly as it came, Wuzzy's brief hesitation disappeared from his face and was replaced with rage. He closed the gap between himself and Richie, and they stood almost nose-to-nose. Richie had to look up at Wuzzy because of the difference in their heights. This brought to my mind an uncanny memory of Hulk Hogan glaring into the dark eyes of Andre the Giant in the main event on my father's *Wrestlemania III* tape.

Richie stood his ground, "Leave him alone, Wuzzy. Or I—"

"You'll what?" Wuzzy interrupted. As he spoke, he puffed his chest out, making himself look even bigger. His face was red with either rage or embarrassment, maybe both.

After he cleared his throat and lifted his chin up defiantly, Richie spoke in a voice so low that I almost couldn't hear him, "I swear to God, Wuzzy, if you even go *near* Shelly, I'll rip your fucking head off."

Wuzzy was taken aback, unbelieving. I looked around the cafeteria and saw that some of the other kids had formed a circle around our table, watching intensely. I found Tiffany looking on as well, wearing a worried face. I put my hand on Richie's shoulder and said his name, hoping to bring him back to his senses, but he shrugged me off and resumed his stare-down with Wuzzy.

Just as Wuzzy seemed to collect his thoughts and was about to say something further or perhaps pummel Richie there and then, Mr. Crawford came through the crowd of students like Moses parting the red sea and yelled, "Break that up there. Break that up right now."

Mr. Crawford hesitated a moment, seeing Richie's face, and then resumed.

"You boys break that up," he said again. "Eddie, go up to the principal's office right now."

Wuzzy ignored him, leaning in and whispering into Richie's ear. Although I couldn't hear it, I could easily read those three words on his lips: watch your back. He turned away and headed toward the principal's office. Mr. Crawford stayed behind a minute to ask us if we were okay. Richie told Mr. Crawford that everything was fine. I just nodded my head, not really believing it. Most of the other students had already gone back to their seats, apparently disappointed that there was no blood. I felt like I had swallowed an eight-pound ball of lead.

*   *   *

I pushed my lunch tray away, not feeling hungry anymore. Some of the color was returning to Richie's face, which looked surprisingly calm. I watched him quietly for a moment, as he absently pushed his french fries around on his tray. I was still trying to figure out what to say when he finally broke the silence.

"He'll be coming for me," he said.

"What were you thinking, dude? What got into you? What're you gonna do?" I unloaded on him.

Richie seemed to either not hear me or ignore me. "He'll be coming for me, Shelly, but I'll be ready."

My mouth dropped open, and I felt like screaming at him. *He'll tear you apart!* But I sensed that he had more to say, so I shut my mouth. His eyes looked cold and detached. I still couldn't believe how calm he was despite his pallor.

"I looked into Wuzzy's ugly eyes. I looked right into them, and you know what I saw in those eyes, Shelly?"

I shook my head. I didn't know.

"I saw doubt, man," he said. "It was there. Doubt."

"Even if that's true, he has friends, Richie. They'll get involved. You embarrassed him in front of everyone."

"No."

"What do you mean *no*?"

"I mean that I challenged him in front of the whole cafeteria, so he'll want to go it alone, I think. And I think I can take him. If I jump on him right away and just start swinging—"

"Have you lost your mind?" I interrupted, my voice cracking on the word *your*. I couldn't believe what I was hearing. First, he mouthed off to the biggest badass in our school, and now he thought he was going to fight him … and *win*? Surprisingly, Richie laughed. "This isn't funny, dude. You didn't need to threaten him like that. It just made things worse."

"Yes, I *did* need to," he explained, "I saw your face, and I snapped."

I sat in silence, waiting for him to continue, not understanding.

"I see that same face every day in the mirror, Shelly. And … and … *goddamn it!*" He threw his plastic fork into his tray in frustration, and it landed with a lackluster clunk.

I didn't know what to say. The Richie I was looking at now was someone I barely knew. He sure looked like my friend Richie, but this guy seemed older and wiser. And *harder*.

He composed himself and went on, "You don't deserve to feel that way. You're a good person, and I won't let Wuzzy do that to you."

"You don't deserve it, either," I said softly. I felt touched by what he said, but I was still concerned for him. I wasn't sure that he was thinking rationally. He leveled his gaze at me, seeming to contemplate what I had just said.

"I don't know. I guess you're right," he said. "That's why I stood up for us. I'm sick and tired of being the fucking punching bag. I don't care about anything else anymore. People are gonna do whatever they want to you in life. I realize that now … but that doesn't mean you have to stand by and let it happen."

"Yeah, I guess."

"That's what I was talking about yesterday. Taking matters into my own hands. Running, Shelly. Running away."

"You were really serious about that? Where would you go?" My mind was racing with questions. "What would you do? You can't just run away like that. You need a plan. And what about me, man? Are you just gonna leave and not look back?"

"You're coming *with* me."

"What?"

"Yeah, why not?" Richie asked. "You've talked about what goes on at your house, man. Is that any way to live? Your parents act like you barely even exist anymore. Hell, I've seen it with my own eyes! They're too wrapped up in their own bullshit to care about you anymore."

The reality of his words gnawed at my heart like a serrated edge. My family had been a picture-perfect slice of American pie before John had died. We had our family vacations and our traditions—our parents letting us open one present each on Christmas Eve and giving us three kisses good night, one for each cheek and one on the forehead. But things had changed when John had died, hadn't they? You bet your ass they had.

John was only sixteen years old when he passed away. It happened two weeks before Christmas in 1990. He had gotten his driver's license a couple months prior and bought himself a used Firebird with $700.00 of his own money. He had wanted a Firebird since he was just five years old, after he had seen a *Smokey and the Bandit I* and *II* double feature. He began saving every little bit of money in a mason jar that he called his "bandit jar." The fifty dollars that he had gotten from grandpa for his birthday every year went into the jar. The thirty-three bucks he had found on the school bus went into the jar. Even the two dimes he had found on the ground under the Second Street pay phone went in the jar, too.

Our parents had dismissed it as a passing phase, assuming he would eventually break down and pour the contents of the jar out on the counter at the candy store or maybe at the toy store for an action figure or two. But by the time I was old enough to remember, his one bandit jar had become two, and by the time he got his license, there were three bandit jars in total.

One day when John's friend Carl was driving me and him home from the movies, John discovered a beat-up black Firebird parked on the front lawn of a Becker Street split-level. It was spotted with rust and strewn with spider webs, adorned with a cardboard sign in the window that read "$750 or b/o."

John flipped his lid and begged Carl to stop the car. After we looked the car over for a few minutes, a husky man with a mullet and an AC/DC T-shirt came out of the house with the keys dangling from one finger. He told John to "start her up," and John was more than happy to oblige. The engine bucked and kicked, and black smoke poured out of the muffler; however, John didn't care. He was in love.

The man knew he had him on the hook and drove the deal home by telling John that he would go as low as $700.00. Because he knew that he had at least *close* to that amount sitting in his bandit jars, John told the man that he would be back and made Carl gun it home. Once there, he jumped out of Carl's car almost before it had stopped and then ran upstairs to his room. He dumped the bandit jars onto his bed and counted $693.43. He borrowed seven dollars from Carl and then swept it all into a pillowcase.

The man wasn't very happy about having to count out a shitload of change from a pillowcase, but he tossed the keys to John and said, "Money is money. Treat her right, kid."

Minutes later, John drove me back home in his clunky Firebird, grinning like the Cheshire cat on cocaine. When we got there, our parents were home. They were a little peeved at first, having hoped that maybe all the money he had saved would go toward college one day, but they warmed up to the purchase soon enough. My father's main concern was that the tires were practically bald, but John swore that he wouldn't drive it in snow storms until he had gotten the tires replaced.

In the days that followed, he drove that car as much as he could; bringing me to the store for no reason at all and driving his friends anywhere they wanted to go. Sometimes he would just sit inside of it parked in the driveway and listen to the radio. When he registered it, he purchased a vanity plate that read "BANDIT." After that, some of the townsfolk took to calling him "the Bandit" when he would drive by, and he was quite tickled when he heard about it from his friends.

Then, one cold night a couple of weeks before Christmas, he was driving back from the movie theater with a carload of his friends and swerved to avoid a baby deer that had run out into the road. During the movie, the temperature had dropped significantly, and patches of black ice had formed on the road. When he swerved, he happened to be on one of those patches, and his bald tires had no chance of gripping the road. Things might have been okay had he been a more experienced driver, but as he began sliding, he slammed on the brakes and steered away from the slide. The car violently spun around twice before it finally smashed into the guardrail in front of the Rockport shoe store.

John's friends told police later that after the crash, he had gotten out of the car clutching his chest, walked a few steps, and then collapsed. By the time help had arrived, John was already dead. The doctor indicated the cause of death as a collapsed lung. His three friends all survived the accident with minor wounds.

Only the Bandit had died.

Christmas that year was cancelled. My parents withdrew, blaming themselves for letting him drive a car with bald tires in the winter. They would ask each other the same questions every night: What were we thinking? How could we be so irresponsible? Then, after a couple of months went by, the questions became more rhetorical: How could he be so stupid? Why did he have to leave us? Why is God so cruel? Finally, the questions had evolved into blame: Why didn't you say anything to him? Why couldn't you have been more of a father to him? Why didn't you just give him the money for the tires? All the while, I was left to fend for myself, alone in my grief, until Richie came into my life.

"Yeah, I know," I said, now looking at Richie. "But it's not like we can just run away. We don't have any money. We don't even have any transportation."

Richie seemed to consider this and then said, "I've been working it all out. I need to figure out how we can get a car, but I know how to drive, dude. That's the *only* good thing I've gotten from Jim, even though the only reason he taught me to drive was because he gets too drunk."

"Okay. Let's say we miraculously got a car. Then what? Where would we go? And what would we do when got there?"

"Well … I've been thinking about Mexico, that way—"

"Are you crazy?"

"—no one will ever find us."

I looked at him for a moment. *Mexico!* He really seemed to have put a lot of thought into this. The look of determination on his face confirmed this notion. His expression seemed to suggest that he had never been as sure of anything in his life as he had been about this.

"You *must* be crazy," I said. "Why not Canada? It's closer. Why Mexico? What the hell is in Mexico?"

"Honestly, Shelly, I don't care. I just want to get out of here. I think Canada is just *too* close, though. We could easily be found there. Plus, we can *work* in Mexico."

"What do you mean?"

"I heard that the minimum working age down there is fourteen. I know you're still thirteen, but we can lie. The bottom line is that I have to get away from Jim. I have to. I don't see any other choice," Richie said. I could see tears forming in the corners of his eyes. He paused, breathing deeply, and then added, "There are just some things I can't tell you about, okay?"

"You mean about Jim? I know that he beats you up, man. And I know that you don't wanna talk about it, but you can. I won't tell anyone."

"There's … more than that. But please, Shelly, I don't want to talk about it. Just trust me when I say that things are horrible and I need to get away."

I sighed, frustrated that he didn't trust me enough to talk about it. "Fine, but what about your mom?"

"Bianca? What about her? Fuck her. She's just as useless as he is, Shelly, you *know* that. I've told you about her."

I then recalled what he had told me about his mother. He may have been fairly tight-lipped about his own interactions with Jim, but he was a little more open about her beatings. He had told me that she was too afraid to do anything. She feared Jim and made excuses for his behavior. After she endured her own beatings, she would often tell Richie, "I love him, you know. We just need to work harder to not do things to make him mad, especially when he's drunk. He works really hard, you know, and he likes to drink when he comes home. It's the only thing that relaxes him. He loves us, you know. I know you don't think so right now, but he really does."

"Still, there must be something you can do besides running away," I said.

"The only other thing I could do is kill him," Richie said. He followed this with a guttural and humorless laugh that made me break out in goose bumps. "But seriously, man, there's nothing else left. I need to get away, and I don't want to do it alone. I *can't* do it alone."

We sat in a contemplative silence for a couple of minutes. I considered the pros and cons of running away. I was intrigued at the thought of being on the road with Richie and getting away from my parents' constant fighting. Plus, it would be my payback for their indifference toward me since John's death—that is, if they even noticed or cared that I was gone. Another good thing was that we would have no rules, no curfews, and no bedtimes. On the other hand, the thought terrified me. I had some money saved up—I hadn't been as dedicated to saving as my brother John had been, but I wasn't too bad off, either—but for how long could that feed and shelter two people? Plus, what if we got caught?

As we sat there in the cafeteria, Tiffany temporarily forgotten about, Richie waited patiently for my answer, fidgeting with his retrieved plastic fork. I began thinking that maybe this was just the beginning of another passing phase. We would probably talk about it for a while and plan things out, but then we would end up focusing on something else in a couple of weeks.

It would be just like when we determined that we needed to form a rock band. We planned for days, filling up several notebooks with possible band names, lyrics, song titles, band logos, album cover concepts, and even fake set lists. We had finally settled on a name, July's Revenge, because we had both been born in July. Once that was established, we wrote that name everywhere. We carved it onto the doors in the restrooms. We wrote it on our notebooks and on other student's notebooks and even on the blackboard before the teacher would get in the classroom. Ironically, neither of us played an instrument, but that didn't stop us from dreaming.

After about a month of that, we had moved on to a different idea, namely starting an all-inclusive music store together. We wanted a place where you could buy CDs and guitars and everything else all in the same place. We filled up some new notebooks, this time with possible store names, drawn-out floor plans, and catchy—at least *we* thought they were catchy—slogans like "Come on down and strike a *chord*" and "What are you waiting for? Just *duet*." Come to think of it, we never *did* settle on a name for our store.

Yes, the more I thought of it, the more I believed that this was just another scheme of ours. I was happy that we would have another project to dive into. *Time to go buy some new notebooks and sharpen those pencils, boys. Get those thinking caps on!* I briefly considered that I could have been wrong or that I was just trying to convince myself that he wasn't serious. Nevertheless, I decided to indulge Richie, and I told him that I would go with him if he really went.

"Are you sure about this?" he asked.

"Yeah, man. Shelton Cole and Richie Kemp, heading down the highway!" I said while I raised the devil horns in the air.

"On the highway to hell!" Richie sang. He was trying to impersonate the late AC/DC singer, Bon Scott, but he sounded more like Marge Simpson. We both cracked up laughing, and I began feeling like everything would be okay. Could I have been more far from the truth?

* * *

I shared the last class of the day, social studies, with Tiffany. Mrs. Sharp was writing out our homework assignments about the American Revolution on the chalkboard. We called Mrs. Sharp "the Nazi" for many reasons, but mostly because she loaded us with more homework than any other teacher. She was thin and small-chested, but she had a wide bottom and fat ankles. I was observing how her big ass jiggled with each stroke of the chalk when Tiffany leaned over and whispered to me, "Is everything gonna be okay?"

"As long as the floor holds out," I whispered back, pointing at Mrs. Sharp's sizeable rump.

Tiffany giggled, and Mrs. Sharp turned around, glaring at all of us. She didn't appreciate laughter in her classroom, which was another reason we called her the Nazi. Luckily, Tiffany and I had returned to what Mrs. Sharp lovingly called the "eyes-front position" before being discovered. When the coast was clear and we could hear the squeak of chalk once again, Tiffany leaned back toward me. As I leaned in to listen, I couldn't help but notice her skirt had ridden up slightly, revealing more of her smooth, milky white thighs.

"I meant with your friend, Richie," she whispered, oblivious to the direction of my eyes. The sweet smell of her perfume was intoxicating. "He really ticked off Wuzzy. Doesn't he realize that?"

After I pried my eyes away from her legs, I whispered, "Yeah, I know. But I think he'll be okay. The principal sent Wuzzy home for the day, so he'll have time to cool off."

"But Wuzzy will be waiting for him after school," she protested, raising her voice a little. This got the attention of Mrs. Sharp again.

"Are you catching flies, Tiffany?" Mrs. Sharp asked.

"No, ma'am," Tiffany said.

"Then keep your mouth closed. One more outburst from you and you will be visiting the principal. Am I clear?"

"Yes, ma'am," Tiffany said. When the Nazi turned back around, Tiffany made mocking faces at her back. Even when she was making those faces, she was still so beautiful to me. She took her notebook out of her backpack and tore out a page. I watched her as she wrote, her head cocked to one side and her tongue absently touching her top lip. I started to wonder what it would be like to make out with her, to have my tongue in her succulent mouth, but then my groin began stirring again. I quickly realized that I had to stop thinking about her, or I would have to walk out of class hunched over with a book in front of my crotch. She finished writing, folded the piece of paper neatly, and held it over to me. I took it, savoring the electric feeling as my finger briefly touched one of hers. I unfolded the note and written upon it in Tiffany's neat script was this:

Shelton:

I know he's your friend, but u should stay out of it. I don't want anything 2 happen 2 u. I think ur really cute ☺ Do u wanna maybe go out with me? I would really like that. Would u? Let me know.

Luv, Tiff

I thought my heart was going to stop. I reread the note a couple of times before it sank in. *She really wants to go out with me!* I then realized I had been holding my breath the whole time and quickly reminded myself to breathe again. I had to resist the urge to jump on top of my desk and scream at the top of my lungs. I peeked over at her and saw that she was anxiously waiting for my reply.

Okay, you gotta play this cool, I thought. I decided that a smooth approach was the best course of action, so I ripped a piece of paper from my own notebook and wrote one word on it: "Yes". Okay, so maybe it wasn't James Bond smooth, but it was the best I could come up with at the time. I was lucky to even remember to breathe.

I folded the note as neatly as I could and held it out to her. I glanced over to see why she wasn't taking it and realized that she wasn't looking at me anymore. She was in the eyes-front position. I also became acutely aware that Mrs. Sharp was no longer at the blackboard. Just as I was about to reel my arm back in, a varicose-veined hand came down and snatched the note from my fingers.

No! I screamed in my head. *It's not supposed to go like this!* I felt panicky as Mrs. Sharp unfolded my note and read it. She looked down at Tiffany with disgust and then turned toward me. I could feel my intestines squirming around like a bucket of worms.

"Mr. Cole, please stay behind after class," Mrs. Sharp said. I swallowed hard with a click and nodded. She appeared very pleased with herself as she pocketed my note and walked back to the front of the class. Tiffany dared a sympathetic glance at me and mouthed the word *sorry*.

I sunk in my chair, deflated. Then I remembered Richie, and a sickening bolt of frantic realization shot through me. Staying after class to be admonished by Mrs. Sharp would prevent me from being able to walk out with Richie, and he would be all alone against Wuzzy. Despite Tiffany's request, I wanted to help Richie in any way that I could, even if all I could do was provide moral support. He had stood up for me; it was the least I could do. But now it seemed like fate was working against me.

* * *

After class, Mrs. Sharp circled around me, glaring as I shuffled my feet and watched the clock. A bead of sweat rolled down the side of my face, even though I felt cold. She removed my note from the pocket of her tight chinos and unfolded it. After she read that one word again, she slammed it down on the desk in front of me.

"What were you saying yes to, young man?" She interrogated.

I thought of the introduction to an older Iron Maiden song called "The Prisoner," which began with a spoken sample taken from a British television show in the 1960s of the same name. "We want information, information, *information* … I am not a number. I am a *free man!*" Despite the situation, a bray of laughter almost escaped me. What saved me was imagining Richie as a bloody pulp lying on the ground, Wuzzy standing over him and grinning like a hunter standing over his kill. That brought me back in a hurry.

"Tiffany was just asking if I thought Mr. Crawford's assignments were tough," I said. If I were to tell Mrs. Sharp the truth, she would surely change our seating arrangements. I couldn't let *that* happen. Sitting next to Tiffany was the only thing that got me through that boring social studies class.

Mrs. Sharp glared at me with narrow eyes. "Is that so? Why are you so nervous, young man? I noticed you keep watching the clock."

I searched my head quickly for another lie and found one. "My mother told me to come home right away after school, because my grandmother is going into surgery and we need to be there when she wakes up."

"Why didn't you just say so?" she asked. It was almost comical how her expression quickly changed from serious to sympathetic. "Go. I can't keep you here knowing that."

"Thank you, Mrs. Sharp," I said, getting up from my chair. "I promise I won't pass notes anymore."

"Oh, don't you go thinking you're clear of this, young man. I'm letting you go today, but we will pick up where we left off after class tomorrow."

I nodded to show that I understood and then quickly stuffed my books in my backpack and walked hastily out of the classroom. When I came out, I was startled to see Tiffany waiting for me. She was leaning up against a locker, and when she saw me, she frantically scrambled over to me. She told me that Richie was headed for the football field.

"That's the worst place to go!" I yelled, remembering how David Sweeney had almost died there at the hands of Wuzzy. I sprang into action, grabbing Tiffany's hand without realizing it, and ran toward the east exit.

* * *

As we carefully ran across the street, Tiffany and I came to the top of the stairs leading down to the football field. The crowd had grown pretty large. I couldn't see Richie and Wuzzy, but I assumed they were in the center of the crowd.

"Come on!" I yelled over my shoulder.

I ran down the stairs toward the crowd, and when I got there, I heard that they were cheering. *Sick bastards*, I thought as I pushed my way through to the front. Just before I got there, a hush fell over the crowd. A terrible thought of Richie lying dead on the ground came to me. Finally, when I broke through, I couldn't believe my eyes.

Richie was sitting on Wuzzy's chest, his knees pinning Wuzzy's arms down. Both of his fists were bloodied, and one of them was held up, poised and ready to strike again. I followed Richie's steely gaze to Wuzzy's face and saw that it was covered in blood. *The proverbial crimson mask*, I thought. There was grass in Wuzzy's hair, and it would have made him look almost humorous if not for the blood.

"Do you give?" Richie asked in a low voice. His hair was messed up more than usual, and he had a cut on his lip with a single drop of blood streaking down his chin. I also saw two small drops above his left eye and realized that it was Wuzzy's blood spatter.

Wuzzy tried to speak, seemingly off in another world. "He's on Dream Street," a boxing commentator might have said. His lips came together and then apart again, forming a crimson bubble of blood and saliva. Then he came to, realizing where he was. When he saw Richie's face, his eyes widened, and he attempted to squirm away. His heels dragged through the grass without purchase, and his fingers clawed at the ground. Richie grabbed the front of Wuzzy's shirt, bringing their faces close together.

"*Do you give?*" Richie screamed into Wuzzy's face.

"Yes! Yes … just … please stop. Please."

Richie let go of Wuzzy's shirt and stood up, chest heaving. I went over to him, and he seemed genuinely happy to see me. We looked around at everyone. Wuzzy's friends and the other bystanders were looking at Richie with a mixture of fear and awe. A grin was starting to form on Richie's face when the crowd began to stir. Tiffany broke through and walked briskly over to us. She told us that we should leave quickly, because some teachers were now coming. I wanted to say something to her, to properly answer the question in her note and make her my girlfriend, but she quickly turned around and disappeared into the crowd. If I had known then that I would never again get that chance, I would have gone after her.

I spared a look back at Wuzzy as I ran to the tree line with Richie. He had rolled over onto his side with his knees to his chest in the fetal position, his whole body hitching and releasing in large sobs. The biggest badass in the school was lying on the ground crying like a baby, and it was my friend that had made it happen. As I heard the story told to me much later in life, Wuzzy stayed that way until every student had left the field, and the teachers had to escort him to the school's infirmary, head hung low.

* * *

Richie and I made it to the trees on the far side of the football field undetected. We walked through the woods in silence. When we were through to the other side, we came out onto Clarence Road. Across the street in the parking lot of the pizza parlor sat a blue Honda Civic with pop music blaring out of the open windows. We stood there for a moment, smoking cigarettes and listening to "Baby, Baby" by Amy Grant while we watched the traffic light change at the intersection of Clarence and Maybrook. After a couple of minutes, Richie spoke.

"I did it," he said plainly. Then he turned toward me, and a huge smile formed on his face. "I fucking did it, Shelly!"

"Yes, you did," I said proudly.

"The shit will hit the fan tomorrow, though. I'll probably be suspended." He paused and then added, "But fuckin' A, it was worth it!"

The teachers and even the principal would be cheering on the inside, having dealt with Wuzzy for years, but they would still have to make an example out of Richie. His actions would be considered punishable by school policy. It just didn't seem fair to me. He was only standing up for himself. If he didn't beat Wuzzy down, then Wuzzy would have pummeled him. Then Wuzzy probably would have pummeled *me* the next day. It was about survival. But the school guidelines didn't take *that* into consideration. The rules simply stated that both students in any fight would be suspended.

41

"I just wish I was there to see it happen, man. I'm sorry about that."

"Hey, no problem, don't worry about it. You had to deal with the Nazi. She's even worse than Wuzzy," Richie said, smiling.

"What happened anyway? How did you get the best of him?"

As Richie told me what had happened, the Amy Grant music from the car ended, followed by Marky Mark and the Funky Bunch, who then gave way to Jesus Jones.

"When I got down the stairs, I ran at him pretty fast," he started. "When I got to him, I was running full-tilt, but then he sidestepped me. And I thought, 'Oh, shit, I'm going face first in the grass.' So I reached out and grabbed a handful of those loose fucking clothes that he wears. I must have grabbed enough, too, 'cause he came tumbling down with me."

"Oh, God."

"Yeah, exactly. That tub of shit landed right on top of me and knocked the air out of me. I thought I was done for, but he landed awkward and rolled. That gave me a chance to roll over onto him and pin his arms down. Once I got up there, I just started swinging. I didn't even feel my knuckles splitting open, Shelly. I just kept punching and punching. Some of my swings even hit the ground, but I didn't care."

His bloody knuckles emphasized this tidbit. I shuddered to think how it felt. Then again, I supposed, Wuzzy probably felt much worse.

"And every time I punched him, I shit you not, his face kept changing from Wuzzy to Jim, from Jim to Wuzzy, and again from Wuzzy back to Jim. I just let it all out on him. The whole time I was thinking about what you said, Shelly."

"What *I* said?"

"Yeah man. You said that I don't deserve being a victim, either. And you were right … so fuckin' right. I fought for me, and I fought for you, and I fought for every fucking person in the world who always gets the shitty end of the stick!"

As he yelled out this last remark, tears balanced in the corners of his eyes, threatening to fall. He wiped at his eyes roughly and shook his head.

"I took that shitty end, and I smeared it all over Wuzzy's stupid fuckin' face. And I don't feel bad about it at all. Is that bad, Shelly?"

"No, I don't think it is. Wuzzy had it coming. I'm just glad I'm friends with the guy who did it," I admitted, laughing. Richie joined in with the laughter and finally looked his age again. The hard look in his eyes had temporarily diminished. Just then, an idea occurred to me.

"Can I ask you something?"

"Okay," Richie said. "But it will cost you."

"Very funny. Seriously though, don't get mad at me, but … did you ever think of fighting Jim? Like, you know, like you just did with Wuzzy?"

Richie stopped smiling and looked off in the distance. I assumed he was contemplating what I had said, so I continued.

"I'm just saying. Wuzzy is kind of … the same size or maybe even bigger than Jim, right? Maybe you could get him to stop hurting your mom and … um … you if you beat him down. Maybe … maybe you could even get him to leave."

As I was talking to him, Richie continued staring at nothing. After a few minutes of uncomfortable silence, he finally spoke. "I don't know, Shelly," he said with a sigh. "I've thought about all kinds of things. Maybe you're right, man. Maybe you're right. But I really don't wanna talk about it right now, okay? It's just that I'm really stoked about kicking Wuzzy's ass, and I don't want to spoil it with talk of Jim, okay? Please?"

"I'm sorry, man," I said. "I'll shut up about it."

We talked for a little longer. The blue Honda Civic had pulled out, and several other cars had come and went. Once we began walking, I told Richie about Tiffany's note and what had happened in Mrs. Sharp's class. Then he told me how he got the cut on his lip; from the zipper of Wuzzy's Starter jacket, of all things. All the while, we wisecracked at each other and swapped arm punches; however, when I next saw Richie, it was under much darker circumstances.

43

PART TWO
PAIN REDEFINED

Chapter 4
DREAMS AND EXPLORATION

October 2008

I had sprawled back down on the lumpy motel bed, hoping to catch another hour or two of sleep, but apparently, it had turned into almost six more hours and another dream—that same recurring dream:

I'm walking down Main Street in Overture. It's a cold night, and there's no sign of life. The town seems deserted. The lights are off in the town hall and in all of the surrounding houses. I forge on, seemingly in slow motion, looking for someone, anyone.

"Where is everyone?" I call out. No answer.

A sinking feeling comes over me. I feel cold, desperate, and alone. I peer into the windows of Christy's Market. The lights are off, and no one is inside. The shelves are empty, and there is a thick layer of dust on the floor and on the counter. It looks as if no one has been in there for years. There are large, intricate webs built in every corner I can see, and the spiders—oh, the spiders—they crawl across the floor toward the window, leaving tiny trails in the dust. They get closer, and I see thousands of tiny black eyes glaring at me accusingly. I back away from the window, and I start to panic.

"Hey! Anybody!" I yell. The only response is my echo.

Lightning flashes overhead, and I look up in time to see the residual light in the sky forming the shape of a greyhound. *How odd*, I think. Then the greyhound moves its head toward me. *Ah, this is a dream*, I finally realize. When I look down from the sky, I see that I am no longer on Main Street. I am standing in front of a house in a field of long grass, surrounded by dark woods. By the light of the moon, I see that it's Richie's house—somehow transported from Calcutta Road to this desolate field. The windows are black with darkness, all except for one. In that one window, there is an eerie flickering light.

I feel terrified and turn away from the house. Behind me, I discover an audience sitting on bleachers that look just like the bleachers on the Overture High School football field. Then I notice that the people in the audience have no mouths, just skin where the mouth should be. They curiously peer at me over their noses.

Behind me, in the direction of the house, an owl asks, "Who?" The sound startles me, and I whip my head around. The audience roars with laughter, and I wonder how they are able to laugh with no mouths. I run toward the house to get away from them. As I get closer, I notice Tiffany on the porch.

She tells me, "You shouldn't have gone. You shouldn't have gone, Shelly. You shouldn't have gone." She repeats it over and over again, sounding almost mechanical. The audience behind me murmurs in agreement. I look back, and I can see in their eyes that they are smiling. They may not have mouths, but their eyes are smiling. I want to scream. When I turn back to the house, my parents are standing with Tiffany. My father's hand is on her shoulder.

"She's right, Shelton. Everything would have been fine if you would have stayed," he says. His hand moves from Tiffany's shoulder down to her breast and slowly massages it. My mother looks on and smiles, as if he were petting a small puppy instead of molesting a young girl.

"What the fuck?" I ask.

Tiffany doesn't even flinch. I see my father smelling her hair and winking at me. Then my mother says to me, "Go on in the house,

Shelton. Richie wants to talk to you. We have to bury Tiffany now. She's starting to smell."

I move forward to the front door, seemingly floating. When I put my hand out to push it open, I notice there's something on my hands. When I hold them up to my face, I see that they are covered in blood. The door then opens by itself, and Richie is in an empty room, sitting in Jim's recliner.

"What's wrong with you, Shelly? It's only a little blood," he says. Then he laughs, and my parents and Tiffany join in. Richie gets up out of the chair and all four of them surround me. Richie whispers in my ear, "He's waiting for you, Shelly, behind the Yankee Flyer."

I close my eyes and scream. I can't help it. I feel terrified. When I open my eyes, the house is gone. The audience is gone, and my parents and Tiffany are all gone, too. It's just Richie and me, and we're standing on some train tracks.

"I don't like it here," he says. He runs into the woods beside the tracks. I follow him, and he stops when he comes to a clearing. It's the train graveyard. "Remember this place?" he asks. I do. I remember it well. "Come on. Let's go a little farther," he says. He runs toward the trail behind the old Yankee Flyer train car. I follow him, running. The woods get thicker and thicker, and finally, there's another clearing with a small lake.

I realize it's not just any lake. No, it's *the* lake.

"No," I say. "Not here—anywhere but here. Please, let's go somewhere else." But it's too late. A dark figure approaches from the trees beside me. He gets closer, and I see his tattoo, the one with the turtle and the three dolphins. I see who it is. Oh, my god, it's him. It's him. It's—

* * *

A vacuum turned on outside of the motel door, jolting me awake. I sat up in the bed, sweating. My eyes squinted against the daylight pouring through the window, and I checked the clock again. This time it was 9:18 AM.

My stomach grumbled loudly. I felt like it would eat itself if I didn't get some food soon. In the shower, I stood there letting the hot water run on my head, watching the night's sweat and dreams swirling around at my feet and flowing down the drain. After I left the motel, I sat in my Volvo for a couple of minutes and thought about where to go before I finally took off.

The motel I was staying at was on the edge of Low Town, so I decided to drive through to the center of town to see how much it had changed—or how much it hadn't. I would then take a drive by Overture High School and my old house. Maybe I would stop to eat at Randy's Diner over on Maybrook Avenue, just fifty feet from where the Honda Civic was serenading us on the day of the fight with Wuzzy. After I ate, I would visit Richie at Hickory Hill. At least that was my plan.

As I drove along Old Shea Road, I reminisced. The lumber mill was on the corner of Old Shea and Crescent, virtually unchanged but for a seemingly new roof. Down a couple of blocks from that was a new street called West Circle Way, which hadn't been here back then. I made a detour down it and saw that it had a brand new development of beautiful modern houses, which was very uncharacteristic of Low Town. Then again, maybe Low Town wasn't so low anymore. As I continued on, I noted that West Circle Way was indeed a half-circle, looping back around to Old Shea Road.

After that, I swung by Richie's old house on Calcutta Road. I parked across the street to check it out. The house wasn't in any better shape now than it had been back then, but on the other hand, it wasn't any worse, which was something. The only major difference was the absence of cars on the blocks. I saw two little black kids run out of the house and around to the side yard. They were laughing and throwing a ball around.

At one point, Richie had told me that the house originally belonged to his mother's great uncle, Maurice. When he died, he left it to Bianca in his will. Richie had said that the news of the inheritance couldn't have come at a better time. Bianca had been having an affair with his father's lawyer while the trial was going on, but after the trial, he lost interest in her and stopped coming around. Bianca had been depressed for months, and Richie had said he pretty much had to take care of himself. Then she got the letter in the mail about the house. She and Richie considered it a chance to start over, so they made the move to New Hampshire.

I remember him telling me how nervous he had been about coming to Overture at first. It was mostly because of his accent, because as a "New Yawka," he tawked like a New Yawka. He didn't want a bunch of small town hicks to make fun of him. Then he met me, and things turned out okay. He had said that those were the best months of his life—that is, until Jim moved in.

As I watched the children playing in Richie's old yard, I thought back to when he had told me about Jim's first meltdown. At first, Richie had explained, Jim was okay. But one night when he was drunk, Richie's mother dropped a glass on the floor while she was doing the dishes, and unfortunately, it broke. Jim was already irritated, because Richie had refused to turn down his music in his room, and he apparently snapped. He hit Bianca and then hit her again when she was on the floor, yelling at her that she had made him do it.

Then he had gone to Richie's room and threw his cassette player out of the window. Richie had said he was furious, because even though he was too poor to have an expensive CD player, his tape player was a higher-end machine, a splurge gift from his father. In fact, it was the only thing he had left of his father. Even though Jim was a lot bigger than he was, Richie said he was brave and pushed Jim in frustration. Jim then backhanded him hard. Richie fell to the floor from the impact, and then Jim punched and kicked him. All he could do was curl up in a ball on the floor to try to protect his face. Richie had later told me that some of the punches that hit his head had formed big, swollen bumps that persisted for a whole week.

He admitted that he had been relieved when Jim finally let up. Apparently, Bianca had come into the room, screaming at him to stop. Once he did, he went to the living room, sat down in his recliner, and drank beer like nothing had happened.

Richie had been so sure that his mother was going to kick Jim's ass out on the street the next day. He wanted to dance around and sing, "Na-na. Hey-hey, kiss him good-bye." But she didn't kick him out. Instead, she made up excuses for him. Things continued on like that, too. Jim would get upset over something and beat Richie or his mother, sometimes both.

Richie confided that one night Jim had beaten Bianca so badly that she had to go to the hospital up in New London. She came home with pain pills, and Richie said that she was a different person from then on, always like a zombie. She eventually became addicted to them, not caring about anything except keeping Jim happy.

What a horrible situation for a kid to be in, I thought as I drove away from the house. *Hopefully, the kids who live there now have it easier.*

I turned down Rhode Island Avenue, which connected to Main Street. Most of the houses looked the same to me, although it had certainly been a long time and it wasn't like I was a connoisseur of architecture. When I turned onto Main Street, I began to see major differences. There were a lot more businesses. There was Brittany's Nail Salon, Brookside Restaurant, and a Citizen's Bank, just to name a few. The biggest surprise of all was the town hall. I had to pull over to the side of the road to get a better look at it.

The town hall had been completely renovated. When I had last seen it, it was an old colonial house with chipped white paint on wooden siding and a small sign out front that read, "Overture Town Hall." There had been an unused, dilapidated barn to the left and a modest gravel parking lot on the right.

Now, the building itself was larger and made of brick, with decorative white cornerstones, lintels, and sills. Above the entrance, a stone tablet with engraved letters read, "Overture Municipal Building." Now, there was a freshly paved and sealed parking lot where the barn used to be. Out front, there was a flag post that boasted the American flag, and underneath that flew the New Hampshire state flag. Notably, the small sign that used to be on the lawn had been replaced by a large, changeable copy-board sign encased in glass. The removable plastic letters spelled out the following:

TOWN ME TINGS TUESDAYS

And beneath that:

OCT 24 2008 STUART ALAN DAY

I couldn't help but be impressed. Our little town hall was all grown up now! I wasn't sure who Stuart Alan was, but I figured he must have done something good to deserve recognition. The new town hall really helped me understand how long it'd been since I had actually set foot in this town. I then pulled away from the curb and continued down Main Street.

Rain started to fall, ticking on the roof and the hood of my Volvo like thousands of tiny drummers working out scores of intricate rhythms. I turned the radio on to drown out the sound, but static poured through the speakers. The station was still tuned to 100.7, which was the Buzzard, Cleveland's rock station. I pressed the seek button, and the first station it came to was Rock 101, the station I had listened to when I had lived here. They were playing a song called "Saints of Los Angeles" from the 2008 Mötley Crüe album of the same name. This brought on a sudden feeling that was an impossible hybrid of déjà vu and *jamais vu*. Here I was, driving through a town that I had lived in as a boy, but it was *not* the same town. And I was listening to a band that I had listened to as a boy, but it was also *not* the same.

* * *

As I headed down School Street, I was relieved to find that the high school hadn't changed. It looked cleaner, but other than that, there were no structural differences. I parked in front of the school, got out, and walked toward the church across the street. I came around the corner to find that the Backyard was empty—no trash cans, no crates, just empty. Then I saw that Christy's Market had been replaced with a 7-Eleven, and I understood. Mr. Underhill wasn't maintaining the Backyard anymore, because he no longer owned the store. What with all the new laws surrounding minors and smoking, the 7-Eleven owners probably wouldn't have seen the gain from the risk.

In my mind's eye, I could see myself and Richie back then leaning up against the brick wall of the church, smoking our Marlboros, and laughing about some silly shit. I could almost feel the quick sting of Richie's punch on my arm. I closed my eyes, and for just a second, I thought I could even smell Tiffany's perfume, even though she had never set foot in the Backyard, not as far as I knew.

I opened my eyes, and there was the present-day Backyard again, still empty. Beyond that, I saw that the vacant lot was no longer vacant. In its place sat a Dunkin' Donuts bustling with Saturday morning customers. A red-headed girl in her early teens emerged from the 7-Eleven with a bag of Doritos. She wore blue jeans and a green top that were both a little too form-fitting for a girl her age.

"Excuse me," I said as she crossed the street and walked past me.

She looked nervously around to see if I was talking to someone else and then yelled, "Get away from me you fuckin' pervert."

"What? No, I'm not a pervert! I just wanted to know if you could tell me when they put that Dunkin' Donuts over there and also about the 7-Eleven, when did—"

"I have mace ... and I'll scream. I mean it," she warned, dropping the bag of Doritos and fumbling through her purse, presumably for her can of mace. I considered how it must have looked to her—a strange, unshaven man coming out of an alleyway wanting to talk to her—and told her I was sorry to have bothered her. As I walked swiftly back toward my car, I thought, *Jesus Christ, what the hell was that all about*? When I got back in the Volvo, I realized I felt guilty for no reason at all. I shook my head and thought how it wasn't just the *buildings* that had changed in this town.

I then drove two blocks to Shriner Way, my old street. I turned down and immediately spotted my old house. Aside from a brand new 2008 Mitsubishi Eclipse parked in the driveway instead of our old '87 Toyota Corolla, the house looked the same. It was still painted yellow and had black shutters. There were still planters under the first floor windows, except whoever lived there now had Petunias instead of Geraniums. As I looked up at the window that had been my bedroom, I wondered what the new occupants of the house had thought when they had discovered the "magic eagles."

When I was six years old, I saw the movie *Dreamscape* and was terrified of the snake man. I was afraid to go to sleep, fearing that the snake man would get me in my dreams. My parents merely told me that it was just a movie and that nothing could hurt me in my dreams, but I didn't believe them. I was six, and I *knew* things.

It was my brother, John, who finally found a way to calm my fears. He told me that he had discovered a way to keep the snake man out of my room.

We sat on my bed while he showed me pictures of eagles in his nature books, and then he pointed to a picture depicting an eagle in midflight clutching a snake in its talons. John explained to me that eagles killed snakes, so snakes were naturally afraid of them. Then he took me into his room and brought out one of his bandit jars from the closet.

"Okay, Shel," he said, fingering through the dollars and coins in the jar. "Now, you know this money is very special to me, right? This is my bandit fund."

I was honored that he even let me *see* one of his precious bandit jars, so I nodded eagerly to show him that I understood.

"Well, open your hand and close your eyes."

I did as he asked, resisting the urge to peek. I heard him rummaging around in the jar and then felt the cold touch of coins filling my little hand. He closed my fingers around them and then told me to open my eyes.

"Now, keep your hand closed to contain the power of what I gave you, and let's go back to your room to seal it off from the snake man."

I followed him back to my room, my fist gripping tightly, not wanting to drop any of his coins. I had the utmost confidence that whatever he was cooking up would work. The only other person who knew more than *me* was my brother John. To me, he was like a wise old sage.

Once we were back in my room, he told me to open my hand. I did so, and I saw that there were six shiny quarters. He told me to turn the quarters over so that the man's face was touching my palm. Once this was done, I now had six noble eagle knights clad in shining silver armor, each ready to protect me.

"Whoa," I exclaimed in my squeaky little voice. "What do we do with them, John?"

"You have to put three on each window sill, Shel. It will only work if *you* do it, so go ahead."

I opened the two windows, put three quarters on each sill, and then closed the windows down on top of them as he instructed. When I was finished, he knelt down and put his hands on my shoulders. He solemnly looked me in the eyes and told me that protecting his little brother was the best buck-fifty he'd ever spent. I threw my arms around his neck and hugged him tightly.

I was never again afraid of the snake man after that.

Tears stung at the corners of my eyes as I looked at our old house. I blinked them away and sniffled. I have never truly gotten over John dying. You never really can fully get over a brother dying. You may move on with your life, and you may even make your peace with it; however, it never leaves you entirely, especially when you think of those private moments you shared together. I turned away from the house, leaving it behind for the last time in my life, and headed for Randy's Diner.

* * *

When I pulled into the parking lot, I saw that Randy's was now called Pippy's Diner. Other than that, the building still looked the same. I headed inside and sat down at the counter in front of a waitress with long brown hair and cute dimples. When she opened her mouth to speak, I saw a big hunk of metal sticking through her tongue. She slithered her tongue around in her mouth, fiddling with the piercing between her teeth as she handed me a menu. If it hadn't been for the bored look on her face, I would have thought she was propositioning me.

After I ordered a coffee, I asked her for an ashtray and pulled out my pack of cigarettes. She pointed at a "no smoking" sign and told me that New Hampshire law no longer allowed smoking indoors. I rolled my eyes and stuffed my pack back in my jacket. *Just great.*

Chapter 5
THE NOTE

September 1991

After Richie and I parted ways that afternoon, I came home to an empty house. I remembered my mother and father bitching that morning because they had to go to some evening wedding. I was relieved about that. I wouldn't have to listen to them yelling at each other all night. I had had enough fighting for one day.

I made my way up to my bedroom and found a note written in my mother's handwriting, attached to a "Strawberries Music & Video" bag. I put the note aside for now and looked in the bag. Inside was the brand new Guns N' Roses CD titled *Use Your Illusion I*. I was touched. My mother hadn't bought me a gift for anything other than my birthday or Christmas since I could remember.

I battled with the cellophane wrapping, eager to see the pictures inside. In their first CD, there had been a drawing of a woman with bared breasts, and in their follow-up one, there had been a *real* picture of a naked woman, though those dastardly black bars had been covering the good parts. No luck this time, though. Despite their promise in the booklet of their second CD that "The loveliest girls are always in your GN'R LP," there was only a collage of live photos in this one. *That's alright,* I thought. *I'm sure the album will be kick-ass anyway*. I put the CD down and found the note, which I had set aside. As I read it, my mood plummeted.

> *Shelton,*
>
> *As you know, your father and I have to go to Dave and Cindy's wedding tonight. We'll most likely be getting home late, so you'll probably be in bed by the time we get home. You better be, it's a school night!!!*
>
> *Anyway, there's leftover lasagna in the fridge that you can heat up for dinner. Just nuke it on high for two minutes. If it's still a little cold, do another thirty seconds. Other than that, your homework and TV should keep you busy. If there is any kind of emergency, call Uncle Bill.*
>
> *By the way, since we won't see you tonight, <u>please,</u> <u>please,</u> <u>please</u> make sure you come home <u>right away</u> after school tomorrow. Your father and I have something <u>really important</u> to discuss with you.*
>
> *Love, Mom*
>
> *PS. I hope you like this CD. The guy at the store said that it just came out, in two volumes. I only bought volume one because I couldn't remember if you like these guys or not. If you do, we can go get the second one this weekend.*

I reread the same line three times, hoping it would change. *Your father and I have something really important to discuss with you.* Closing my eyes, I could feel my heart hammering in my chest like a car stereo in the ghetto. *This is it. They are finally going through with a divorce*, I thought. Until now, I had always thought that I wouldn't give two shits either way about them getting divorced, considering how they treated me like I was invisible most of the time. But now that it was actually happening, I was deeply hurt and angry. We had already lost one member of our family, and now they wanted to split us apart even further? And just *who* am I supposed to live with? And what will everyone else think of us? Despite my feelings about my parents, they were all I had left of John, and they were all I knew of "home."

I crumpled the note up into a ball and flung it across the room, but that didn't feel like enough. A wicked rage was tearing through me, and I wanted to break something. I picked up the new Guns N' Roses CD and hurled that into the wall. The corner of the case connected with the wall, instantly snapping the plastic and causing the tray to separate from the cover. The disc spilled out onto the floor, landed on its edge, and rolled across the floor until it hit the bottom of my dresser, at which point it flopped over.

As I stared at the broken case and motionless CD by the foot of my dresser, my rage dissipated and morphed into a heavy sorrow, and I began to cry. I cried for myself. I cried for my parents, for John, and for Richie. I even cried because I felt bad for throwing and breaking my mother's thoughtful gift. I just stood there and cried.

Then I sat down on the bed and cried some more.

Sometime later, after I had rubbed my eyes raw, I stopped. I shuffled downstairs, heated up the leftover lasagna, and sat on the couch to eat it. I surfed through the channels, looking for *Seinfeld*, but it wasn't on. I found *The Cosby Show* instead, which lifted my spirits somewhat. Assaulted by a barrage of commercials,

("*I've fallen ... and I can't get up!*")

my thoughts drifted to my parents and what it would be like to have two Christmases. The thought didn't appeal to me. Then *The Cosby Show* came back on, and I watched Clair demand to know why Vanessa had kept her relationship with Dabnis a secret for this long. During the next block of commercials,

("*Choosy moms choose Jif.*")

I thought of Richie again and wondered what was going on over at his house. I watched television off and on like that for over an hour, picking at my lasagna as it got cold.

After I put my dish in the sink, I went back upstairs to my room and inspected the Guns N' Roses CD. It had survived my rage without a scratch. Perhaps that was a small favor from God, but why couldn't He just give me one *big* favor instead? *Make my parents stay together.*

I put the CD in the player and listened to the music as I attempted to complete my homework assignments. Soon after that, I fell asleep. During the night, I slightly awoke as I heard my parents come home. I thought I heard them giggling as they came up the stairs, but that was obviously a dream. They wouldn't be giggling like that. They were getting a *divorce*. It was probably my mother crying again.

My mind filled with maybes. Maybe she would stop crying if I ran away with Richie. Maybe they wouldn't get divorced if I left. *Maybe that's what they're hoping for,* I thought. *Maybe they want me to leave.*

Both sad and angry, I fell back asleep and dreamed that John was still alive and that our family was happy again.

* * *

When I woke up the next morning, I discovered my mother had gone to work early as she sometimes did. Downstairs, my father was sitting in his usual chair at the kitchen table and reading the newspaper. I walked over to the kitchen counter and submerged a pair of Pop-Tarts in the toaster. When he peered over his newspaper, my father began to speak to me.

"Hey, kiddo, how was your night?"

How long had it been since he had called me kiddo? *Quite some time,* I thought. I noticed his eyes were slightly bloodshot and he had stubble on his face. I couldn't believe he was planning on going to work like that, but then again, I didn't really care.

"It was okay," I said. "Why didn't you shave?"

"Oh?" He ran his fingers down the side of his face, which made a sandpaper sound. "Guess I forgot. I had a couple drinks at the reception last night. I have quite the headache this morning to pay for it."

Incredibly, he winked at me, and a small chuckle escaped him. I couldn't believe he was acting like everything was fine! *You're about to rip our lives apart, you asshole! How can you sit there giggling like a fucking little girl?* I felt the rage from the night before building up inside of me. I could barely hold back the urge to punch him in the mouth.

60

Just then, the Pop-Tarts popped up, and I yanked them from the toaster, barely feeling them burning my fingers as I wrapped them in a paper towel. Then I snatched up my backpack from the floor and headed for the door, trying to get outside before I blew up.

My father called out to me, "Hey, where are you going so early?"

"I have to go to school early today, because I'm helping to set the gym up for a pep rally," I lied. I stopped walking, but I didn't turn around. I was afraid that if I looked my father in the eyes right then, I would have either cried or lunged at him. Thankfully, he didn't press the matter.

"All right, just make sure to come home right away after school. You're mother and I have made some decisions about some things, and we want to discuss them with you as a family."

"Yeah ... I know," I muttered and then shoved the screen door open and flew down the front stairs. I ran the whole way to the Backyard. When I arrived there, Nick Driscoll and Brett Taylor were loitering about, smoking cigarettes and shooting the shit. I hurriedly dragged my arms across my eyes to dry them as I approached. I stopped a couple of feet short of them and lit a cigarette, acting cool. They continued their conversation after they greeted me with a nod. I nodded back and took a long drag off of my cigarette. That was when I heard the sound of squealing tires coming from behind me.

That was when my life changed forever.

Chapter 6
PREPARATIONS

September 1991

I whipped my head around to see who was squealing their tires at Christy's, wishing that Richie were here so we could laugh together when Mr. Underhill came running out of the store to bitch at whomever it was. Then I noticed that the car was familiar. A chill travelled down my spine when I realized it was Jim's IROC-Z. According to Richie, it was Jim's most prized possession. He called it "Cherry," because it was painted candy apple red. Richie had told me that he had fantasized about smashing it with a baseball bat on many nights.

I looked around, wondering where I could hide if Jim were to come toward me. I saw Nick and Brett looking curiously at the urgency clearly plastered on my face. I heard someone yelling my name from the car, and I had to squint my eyes to see that it was Richie. A wave of relief swept over me, which was quickly followed by confusion. Why would Richie be driving Jim's car? He called my name again, and I ran across the street to talk to him.

"Shelly, I'm so glad you're here early," Richie shouted in a cracking voice.

"Dude, why are you in Jim's car?" I asked. Then I noticed the blood on his shirt. "What happened? Are you bleeding?"

"I'll tell you later. Just get in," he urged.

"What are you talking about? We have school. We have—"

"Never mind school. Please, Shelly, just get in. We have to get out of here now," he yelled.

I briefly hesitated and then walked around to the passenger side and got in the car.

"Okay, I got in. Now would you just tell me what's going on?"

"We'll talk on the way," Richie said as he stepped on the gas and peeled out of Christy's. In Cherry's side mirror, I saw that Mr. Underhill had just burst out of the store, ready for action. I put my seat belt on and grabbed the "oh, shit" handle.

"Well? Where are we going?" I asked, beginning to feel frightened.

"To your house to pack your things," he said.

As he was saying this, I noticed the bags in the backseat, and a dawning realization set in. We arrived at my house two streets over, and he pulled into the driveway. My father had gone to work already, so the Toyota was gone.

"What the hell happened, Richie? I'm not getting out until you tell me."

"There was an accident," he said, looking absently out the window.

If not for the blood on his shirt, I would have thought he was playing some distasteful joke on me. I asked him, "What do you mean? Richie, what happened? Are you okay?"

Sighing, he said, "I don't have time to tell you all of the details right now, but I stood up to Jim just like I did with Wuzzy. Just like you told me to do, man."

"But ... what happened? Did you beat him up?"

"He was gonna kill me, Shelly. I know it. I didn't have a choice. I just didn't have a choice—" He choked up and began to cry.

I was confused and afraid. I didn't know what to make of what he was saying, but I knew it had to be bad if it was making him cry. "What didn't you have a choice about, Richie?"

"It was an accident, man," he said between sobs.

"What was an accident?"

63

"Jim's dead. He's dead, Shelly."

"What? Did you … did you kill him?"

He nodded slowly. "But I didn't mean to. He was going to kill me." He buried his head in his hands and repeated it again through sobs. "He was going to kill me."

I listened with growing horror. My friend had killed someone. He had committed *murder*. I tried to take the fact that it had been self-defense into consideration. That helped me accept the situation a little, but I knew that I would probably never look at Richie the same again.

Nothing would ever be the same again.

I put my hand out to console him and then pulled it back. *What's wrong with you?* I thought. *He's still Richie. He's still your friend.* I put my hand out again, and this time, I put it on his shoulder. I could feel him trembling. *What else could he have done? If Jim was trying to kill him, he had no choice. Just like he said.*

He wiped his tears and spoke softly to me, reminding me of our conversation; that I had agreed to run away with him. He told me that going with him was the only reason he knew things would be okay, that we could start a new life, and that things would get better. When he finished, I sat in silence, listening to the hum of Cherry's engine. I didn't share his enthusiasm about running away, but I wasn't altogether against it, either. Mostly, I felt responsible for what had just happened. After all, I was the one who had suggested only yesterday that Richie should fight Jim. I could hear my own words repeating in my head over and over: *Maybe you could get him to stop hurting you and your mom if you beat him down. Maybe you could even get him to leave.* Pangs of guilt flowed through me. How could I tell him no?

I also wasn't sure that I wanted to stick around tonight to hear my parents tell me that they are getting divorced, knowing that if it had been me inside that coffin instead of John, the family would probably remain together.

Don't think that way, Shel, I heard John's voice say in my head. *They love you. They're just too wrapped up in themselves to show it right now.* I strongly doubted it. Besides, John was dead. *Why should I listen to him now?* He had left me alone to suffer.

I didn't want my parents to get divorced. I didn't want to be tossed back and forth between two houses. *What kind of life is that?* But there was nothing I could do about any of that. As John used to say, "You can wish in one hand and shit in the other, and you'll see which one fills up first."

I looked at Richie, who kept checking the rearview mirror and glancing out the windows for police cars, and felt a kind of warmth. Here was my best friend—no, my brother—sitting there and asking me to come with him, baring his soul to me, asking me to help him get away from what was happening. He was the only person left in the world who gave a shit about me and surely the only one who made me feel like I was worth anything.

"Okay," I said.

Richie looked away from the rearview mirror and peered into my eyes with obvious relief.

"Richie and Shelly versus the world, right?" He asked, holding his hand out to me.

I grabbed his hand, shook it, and said, "Richie and Shelly versus the fucking *universe*, man."

He smiled gratefully and told me to quickly pack as many clothes as I could and to find as much money as I could possibly lay my hands on. He paused and then told me to grab a highlighter as well. I got out of the car and ran into the house. With Richie's advice in mind, I dumped out the contents of my backpack and filled it with as many clothes as I could. I pulled down the shoe box containing my modest savings and folded the bills before I stuffed them in the front pocket of my backpack. There was only $105.00 there, but it was better than nothing. In my parents' bedroom closet, I found my father's gym bag and began filling that with clothes as well. In the bathroom, I packed my deodorant, toothbrush, and toothpaste. I thought about it for a second and then grabbed a couple of rolls of toilet paper, too.

Back in my room, I spotted Tiffany's note folded neatly on my dresser, and I stuffed it in my pocket. I then grabbed a handful of

CDs to listen to on the road. Downstairs, I grabbed a highlighter from my father's study and glanced around to make sure I wasn't missing anything. Weighed down with the heavy bags, I crossed the living room toward the front door. I stopped by the phone and looked at it for a minute, considering a phone call to my mother or father. Maybe they could sit down with us and help us figure out a better solution. I eventually decided against that option, but instead, I grabbed a pen and wrote a note:

> *Mom and Dad,*
>
> *I don't have much time, but I just wanted to tell you that I love you guys. I know you're getting a divorce and I hate it. I wish you guys would stay together. I know you wish I was dead instead of John, but I can't help that.*
>
> *Anyway, something happened with Richie. I'm sure you'll find out about it soon in the news. So he came to get me, and we're leaving. I can't tell you where we're going, but maybe you guys can stay together now that I'm gone. I love you.*
>
> *- Shelton*

I signed the note, locked the front door of the house, and got into Jim's stolen IROC-Z after I threw my bags in the backseat.

"What the hell took you so long? They could already be looking for me," Richie said as he burned out of the driveway.

"I wanted to make sure I didn't miss anything. What's the highlighter for?"

"It's for this," Richie said, handing me a pocket-sized book titled *1991 United States Road Atlas*. "I found it in Cherry's glove compartment. Highlight us a route from 89 South all the way down to Mexico, Shelly. We're movin' out."

My mind was racing, and my stomach was turning. I couldn't believe we were actually doing it. Richie and I were running away.

PART THREE
BRAVE NEW WORLD

Chapter 7
HIGHWAY TO HELL

September 1991

Two hours later, we crossed the Massachusetts state line and exited the highway in a small town called Bernardston. I was filled with excitement, dread, and worry. As we got further away from Overture, the intensity of these feelings increased. I wasn't sure if I had made the right choice or not. Then again, I wasn't sure I had made the *wrong* one, either. However, I was convinced that *Richie* had made the right decision. I could just imagine how many cop cars and news vans would be parked along Calcutta Road back in Overture. If Richie had stayed, he would have been arrested and made into a spectacle.

During the two hours from New Hampshire to Massachusetts, Richie explained everything. He finally opened up and confirmed what I had already suspected: Jim was not just violent toward Richie's mother but also Richie. In fact, Richie admitted, Jim beat him more often. He then filled me in on the details of what had happened last night.

He said he had been afraid to go home to Jim, because the school had mostly likely called home to report the fight with Wuzzy. Even if they hadn't, he knew that Jim would eventually see the cuts on his knuckles and he would find out that way. Either way, it meant a potential beating, especially if Jim was drunk.

"So, what did you do then?" I asked.

"When I came around the corner of my street, I saw him in the driveway. He was tinkering around under Cherry's hood and singing along to his fucking Lynyrd Skynyrd. There was one beer on the roof of the car, and there were like seven empty ones on the ground."

"So he was probably drunk by then?"

"Yeah, for sure. So I just froze there, man. I felt good about beating up Wuzzy, you know? I didn't want to ruin it by getting beaten up by Jim again. Plus, I knew I would probably fight back this time like you told me to."

I felt another pang of guilt and tried to ignore it. "Did he see you?"

"Luckily, no. He was focused on whatever he was fixing or adjusting on the car. So I ran. I didn't know what else to do. I just kept running and running. The whole time I was thinking about that movie with Michael Landon. What was it? *The Loneliest Runner,* I think."

"I never saw it."

"Aw, man. This kid our age was a bed wetter, and his mother would hang his piss-stained sheets out the window for everyone to see as punishment. So, he would run home from school every day to get ahead of the other kids and bring the sheets in before they could see on their way by."

"What does that have to do with anything?" I asked.

"I don't know, man. Give me a break. My mind is racing a hundred miles an hour here."

"Well, where did you go?"

"I finally stopped when I got to the woods out behind the lumber mill," he said.

I nodded, remembering the place. He and I had gone out to the lumber mill to hang out several times that summer. We would climb around on the wood piles when the workers weren't around and then jump off. Sometimes we went into the woods to smoke butts and explore.

"I went over to that big-ass maple tree we found and sat down to think about what I should do, and then I decided to read that book for Ms. Pender's class, since I had my backpack."

"Ugh," I grunted. Ms. Pender had assigned a book report on *Pride and Prejudice* by Jane Austen. I hated old books. I was more interested in Stephen King and Dean Koontz.

"After a while, I fell asleep. I didn't mean to. But I woke up later, and it was quarter to midnight."

"Holy shit, you slept in the woods for that long?"

"Yeah, I was fucking cold when I got up, too. So anyway, I ran home and saw the living room light on, but luckily it was my mother who was up. I stood there for a couple minutes, looking at her through the window and watching her pop her pain pills."

"So, Jim was sleeping then?"

Richie nodded. "When I came in, I could hear Jim's snoring. My mom came up to me all whispery and asked me where I had been. She said the school had called about the fight with Wuzzy and she wanted to know what that was all about."

As Richie spoke, I was impatient to find out what had happened with Jim, but I didn't want to push him too hard. At the same time, I almost didn't want to know. I wasn't sure I wanted to hear the details about how my friend had just murdered someone, but I supposed it was necessary. If Richie and I were to continue being friends and continue on the road together, I felt there should be no secrets between us. I was sure I had read in a book somewhere that secrets could be dangerous.

"I told her, 'I stood up to a bully, ma. Something you should learn to do.' And then she slapped me in the face, man."

"That sucks."

"And it's not like the actual slap hurt me much. I've felt much worse pain from Jim, but it hurt a lot on the *inside*, you know?"

I nodded. Richie was already a punching bag for Jim; he didn't need his mother hitting him, too.

"But anyway, I asked her if she could just not tell Jim about the school calling, and she told me that Jim was the one who had picked up the phone."

"Oh, fuck," I said.

"Yeah, exactly. So, I decided to just go to bed and not think about it anymore. And when I started going upstairs, my mom told me that she loved me."

His eyes welled up with tears again, and he let out a heavy sigh.

"You okay, dude?" I asked when I saw his bottom lip quivering.

He nodded and blinked away his tears. "I just feel bad, 'cause I just kept walking up the stairs. I didn't say, 'I love you,' back to her, man. I never even turned around. I just … I think I'm gonna regret that for the rest of my life, you know?"

"Yeah."

"She's not perfect, but she's still my mother. If I'd have known that we were leaving today, that I'd never see her again, I would have told her that I love her."

I thought about my parents and wondered when I last told them that I loved them. I couldn't remember. It had been a while.

"I think—"

"Oh, shit, fuck, shit," Richie shouted as he looked in the rearview mirror. His face drained of its color, and his eyes were wide.

"What? What is it?" I asked, whipping my head around to see what he was looking at. My heart almost stopped when I saw a police cruiser pulling out from an access road, his lights flashing. He was moving toward us very fast. "Oh, my God, Richie."

The cruiser weaved in and out of traffic and then pulled up right behind us, riding close to Cherry's rear bumper. According to the speedometer, Richie wasn't speeding, so I assumed that it had to do with Jim. Richie and I glanced at each other. He looked as terrified as I felt. Our trip would be over before it had even begun.

He switched to the right lane and prepared to pull over. Then, as if it were divine intervention, the cop passed us on the left side. We watched in shock as he sped by without even glimpsing at us.

"He's after someone else!" Richie yelled. He chuckled with relief, and I joined in soon after. We didn't talk for a few minutes after that, still stunned from the close call. Farther down the road, we saw that the cop had pulled some poor schmuck over and was now standing at the driver's window, a ticket book in his hand.

I thought back to when Richie had confided in me about the night his father had been arrested. Obviously, it had been very traumatic for him. Richie had only been twelve years old when it had happened. His mother had been cooking dinner, and his father had been sitting on the couch next to him. They were watching a new show called *Tales from the Crypt*.

A forceful knock at the door startled the Gallo family that night. That was when they noticed the flashing lights seeping in the room around the edges of the window shades. Richie's father stood up and began yelling at Bianca to call the lawyer. The cops shouted from outside the door, "NYPD. Open the door. Dino Gallo, we have a warrant for your arrest. Open the door now." Dino opened the door, and a swarm of policemen entered their home. They handcuffed Dino and conducted a search of the premises. One of them found a handgun and said, "Bingo." Then they took him away while Bianca screamed and cried. It was the last time Richie ever saw his father as a free man.

Richie had admitted to me that ever since then, he got nervous when he saw cops. It always made him think of the scared look on his tough father's face as he was taken away. He had told me that he hated the police for that reason, and now he had an even bigger reason to be afraid of them.

I tried to imagine what was going through his head as we passed the officer giving the ticket. I didn't know what to say. I just waited for him to continue, staring at Jim's keys swinging back and forth from the ignition. There was a key chain attached, which read, "Lost your cat? Look under my tires."

Finally, he broke the silence. "So now I guess I have to tell you what happened in the morning. I've been kinda stalling, man. It's just not easy to talk about."

"I understand, dude. Take your time."

"Thanks," he said. After a sigh, he began, "So, my alarm clock went off in the morning, and when I opened my eyes, there was Jim hovering over me with a crazy look in his eyes."

I shuddered. *What a scary way to wake up,* I thought.

"He said, 'Good morning, you little bastard. Your mother's gone, and it's just me and you.' Then he grabbed me by the hair and yanked me out of the bed and dragged me past the stairway and into the bathroom."

"Oh, God, Richie."

"Then he yanked me up by my shirt and pushed my face into the mirror and started yelling in my face, telling me I'm a fucking failure and I should never have been born and I'm nothing but trouble."

I closed my eyes. *This is terrible,* I thought.

"His face was so close to mine that I could smell the sour stench of night-old beer on his breath, too. It made me want to puke."

"Yuck."

"So, uh … after that is when he tried to kill me."

"Well, what did he do?"

"He … uh, he was behind me and … uh, he started choking me. Yeah. And I started panicking, and then I remembered what you said. I took care of Wuzzy, so that means I can take care of Jim."

"Yeah," I said. I wished I had never said that bit about Wuzzy to him.

"So I slammed my head back into his face. I must have broken his nose, too, because there was a lot of blood gushing out from between his fingers and he was screaming in pain. I didn't want to give him any time to think, though, so I turned around and kicked him in the balls as hard as I could."

"Oh, my God. What did he do?"

"I didn't give him time to do anything," Richie said. "I pushed him backward into the shower. The fucker took the whole shower curtain with him, too. And then I turned to run out of the bathroom, but I wasn't fast enough. He lunged out of the tub and grabbed my ankle, making me fall face first on the floor."

I tried to imagine what I would do in the same situation. I didn't think I would have been as strong and brave as Richie had been. I probably would have panicked. And perhaps begged.

"But I was running on instinct or something man, 'cause I got up wicked quick and started running again. And just as I got to the top of the stairs, the motherfucker tackled me, and I fell to the floor again. And he landed right on top of me. Knocked the air right out of me, too."

I cringed, imagining the impact.

"Then he got right up and stood over me with the blood from his nose dripping all over me and told me he was going to kill me for what I just did." Richie honked the horn at the car in front of us. "Aw, come on, dude. Speed up!"

He quickly checked his mirror and his blind spot and then swung around to the passing lane. As we passed the car, we saw the old man driving shaking his head. I glanced at the speedometer and saw that Richie was going 80 mph. Recalling the details of his fight with Jim was definitely taking its toll on him.

"Dude, calm down," I said. "He wasn't going that slowly. There could be another cop up here somewhere, too."

"Sorry. So where was I? Oh, yeah, so he grabbed my shirt and lifted me up, and I tried kicking him in the balls again. He caught my foot this time, and that made me fall back on the floor *again*, this time on my ass."

He changed lanes again and dropped his speed back down, which helped me breathe a little easier.

"I couldn't believe it, man. I thought I was dead for sure. He knew he had me, too. Even though I had broken his nose and kicked him in the balls, he actually laughed. That scared the fuck out of me."

"Jesus, what happened then?"

"Well, he still had my foot in his hand, and he leaned in to say something to me, so I brought my other leg up and put it on his chest and pushed as hard as I could to get him away from me. Then it was just crazy, man."

He paused to light up a cigarette and took a long drag before he finally continued. "My kick knocked him back, but he was still holding on to my foot with one hand. Then my sock came off in his hand, and he lost his balance. I didn't even realize that his back was to the stairs until I saw him fall backward."

"So he fell down the stairs?"

"Yeah, he fell backward and tumbled all the way down like a sack of shit. It made a horrible sound. I couldn't believe it. I didn't mean to, Shelly. I didn't mean to kill him." He hesitated for a moment, fighting back more tears and focusing on the road. "But even though I didn't mean it, I'm not sorry for it."

"What—"

"I know that probably sounds bad," he interrupted. "But I don't care. I didn't really have a choice, you know? I was defending myself." He flicked his cigarette out of Cherry's window and then continued, "But I was so scared, Shelly. I've never seen someone's eyes look so crazy like that. If it wasn't for my sock falling off, I would be in a coffin right now instead driving down the highway."

I shuddered at the thought. "Jesus, man," I muttered. I was still trying to wrap my head around the whole thing. It was all too surreal. *Richie killed somebody.* I knew he would never hurt me, but at the same time, I was a little frightened.

"I really didn't think he would fall down the stairs when I pushed him. I really didn't. But you know what, man? I'll always remember the look on his face when he fell backward. He looked scared, Shelly. That piece of shit motherfucker was scared. And even if he didn't die, even if he had gotten back up and killed me, I probably would have died happy, you know? To see fear on that bastard's face just once. You don't know what that did to me, Shelly. You just don't know."

Richie trailed off, slowly shaking his head. I watched him in silence. I tried to imagine what he meant about dying happy, but it was beyond me. The only thing I could think of was when Darth Vader threw the emperor into the abysmal power shaft, freeing himself of the dark side and saving his only begotten son in the process. Darth Vader died happy that he was able to sacrifice himself for the greater good and to look his son in the eyes for the first time.

"Did you check his pulse?" I asked once I was sure that Richie had finished talking.

"No, I didn't. But if you would have seen the way he fell, you would know that I didn't need to. Like I said, he must have broken his neck. Especially the way he landed. If he was alive, I think he would've been screaming. He didn't move at all for however long it took me to pack up my shit. He was dead, Shelly. No question about it."

I took his word for it. The only dead person I had ever seen had been my brother, but that was after he had been embalmed and covered with postmortem makeup. Even then, I got the feeling that he would just sit up in his coffin and say, "Hey, Shelton!"

We sat in another short silence, Richie concentrating on the road and me looking out the window, watching the trees on the side of the highway fly by. I was surprised to learn that Richie was a pretty good driver. I had glanced at Cherry's speedometer several times and had seen Richie maintaining the speed limit the whole time. Considering the scare we experienced with the cop earlier, Richie needed to be extra careful. He was an unlicensed driver, he had just committed murder, and he was a minor to boot. He needed to make sure to obey the traffic laws to avoid being pulled over.

He had told me one time at school that Jim had taught him to drive. There were several nights when the bartender at Gill's Sports Bar would confiscate Jim's keys and call the house for someone to pick him up. Being the only sober person in the house, because his mother was hopped up on pain killers most of the time, Richie had to hoof it to the center of town so he could drive Jim home.

He had explained Jim's unorthodox teaching methods with a grimace. Evidently, Jim would wallop Richie on the side of the head if he pressed the brake too hard or gave it too much gas taking off. Slurring and drooling, he would tell Richie that a car was like a woman, you needed to "give her a stiff one and she'd open right up for you." Then Jim would throw his head back and laugh like a hyena. I found it ironic that Richie was putting those skills he had learned from his stepfather to good use after he had just killed the man.

"So then what? You packed up your shit and just left?" I asked.

"I stared at his body from the top of the stairs for a couple of minutes before snapping out of it and packing up. I also went into my mother and Jim's room and pilfered Jim's wallet."

"How much did you grab?"

"He had five hundred and sixty-eight dollars in there."

"Wow, that can probably get us all the way to Mexico."

"That's what I figure. I also stole a full carton of his cigarettes and obviously his car keys. Then I left the house." He paused and then continued, "I had to step over his body at the bottom of the stairs, though. Scared the shit out of me."

"Yeah, I bet."

"I kept thinking he was gonna jump up and grab my ankle or something."

I was amazed at Richie's bravery. In the same situation, I didn't think I would have been able to keep my head straight like that. I pictured myself curled up in a ball and crying. Then again, maybe I wasn't giving myself enough credit. Whenever I was being a wimp about something, John used to tell me that he can see a big brave man inside me just dying to get out.

"Well, my night and morning weren't as crazy as that," I said, breaking the momentary silence. "But my mother left me a note last night when they went to that wedding. She wrote that her and my father had to talk to me about something very important. Obviously, they're getting a divorce."

"Probably," Richie replied. He seemed very grateful to be off the subject of Jim. "You said it was just a matter of time, right?"

"Yeah, they had talked about it already." I laughed and then added, "Actually, they *fought* about it is more like it."

"Who do you think would have gotten custody of you? Probably your mother, right?"

I thought about it for a second and then said, "I really don't give a fuck to tell you the truth. It's not something I need to think about anymore."

"Damn right."

"She *did* buy me a nice little consolation prize, though," I said with a twinge of guilt. I pulled out the Guns N' Roses CD. "Wanna crank out some tunes?"

"Fuck, yeah," Richie said.

I loaded the disc in Cherry's player. We bobbed our heads to the music at first, but soon, we were banging our heads and attempting to sing along. That was the comfort that Richie and I had together. We could be ourselves around each other.

* * *

"Why are you getting off the highway?" I asked as he was slowing down on the exit ramp in Bernardston, Massachusetts.

"We're gonna kill two birds with one stone," he said.

"Haven't you done enough killing for one day?" I asked, trying to maintain our usual humor in light of the situation. I immediately regretted saying it, though.

"I'm gonna add *you* to the list in a second," he said chuckling. I didn't say anything, but that frightened me a little. It must have shown on my face, too, because he cleared his throat and apologized. "I'm sorry, dude. You know I didn't mean anything by that, right?"

I nodded.

"So anyway … we need gas, and we also need to get rid of this license plate."

"Get rid of the license plate?" I asked, perplexed.

"You're starting to sound like a fuckin' parrot," Richie teased and then punched me in the arm.

After the punch, he pulled his hand back and shook it in pain. He had used the fist with the injured knuckles, hurting himself in the process. I laughed heartily at this, and he joined in soon after. At that moment, I decided that even though what Richie did to Jim was scary, it was an accident. And apparently, Jim had it coming. Richie was my "brother from a different mother," as we liked to say, and I needed to be there for him, especially because I was the one who had told him to fight back.

When the laughter died down, he told me how people on the run in movies would switch license plates with other cars to avoid police detection. That way, he explained, we could go farther without having to worry, because they would be looking for a red IROC-Z with Jim's license plate, not a red IROC-Z with *another* license plate. I was amazed at how much thought Richie had put into this. There I was yesterday, thinking that this would be just another Shelly-and-Richie phase, but here we were today in some town I'd never heard of on our way to Mexico.

"Where are we going to steal someone's license plates?" I asked.

"I haven't thought of that yet," he admitted. "I'm gonna look for a parking garage or something like that where most people aren't watching their cars."

We didn't find a garage, but I saw signs for a campground and suggested that to Richie. He followed the signs to the Purple Meadow Campground and pulled in. There were plenty of cars to choose from in the lot. As we cruised through the aisles, we noticed only one couple getting out their car and walking toward the interior of the campground.

Richie parked next to a white Chevy Blazer and got out of the car. He opened Cherry's hatch and clanked through Jim's toolbox until he found a flathead screwdriver. I got out and stood watch while he switched the license plates with the Blazer. The whole operation took about five minutes, and then we were back on the road, heading toward the gas station we had seen when we had gotten off the highway.

While I pumped gas, Richie changed into a blue Yankees T-shirt. As a Red Sox fan, it was hard for me to refrain from getting on his case, but he had been through enough already that morning, so I let it slide. He threw his blood-riddled shirt in the trash by the pump and sneered at it in disgust. He muttered about how careless it was that he had waited until now to get rid of it. If anyone had seen him, a young boy with blood all over his shirt, it would have been all over for us. We decided to start being more careful. In that spirit, we figured it would be better for me to go in to pay for the gas in case they had pictures of Richie on the news already.

Inside, I walked over to the cooler to get us some Cokes. Nervousness crept over me, because I thought I could feel the store clerk's eyes burning a hole in my back. I dared to look at him as I picked up a bag of chips. He was a middle-aged man with bushy eyebrows, wearing a green and yellow John Deere hat. I was relieved to see that he wasn't paying any attention to me whatsoever. He was sitting behind the counter, reading a Stephen King book called *Different Seasons*. I told myself I was just being paranoid and wiped the sweat on my forehead as I brought the chips and Coke to the counter.

"Skippin' school, are ya?" The store clerk asked. He was grinning, and I noticed the unmistakable bulge of chewing tobacco in his cheek.

"N-no," I uttered.

"S'alright, kid, I ain't gonna tell. Anyhow, that's ... uh, two ninety-nine for the Cokes and chips and looks like an even twenty-five for the gas. That brings the total to twenty-seven dollars and ninety-nine cents." He put my purchases in a paper bag and palmed my twenty-eight dollars.

"Thanks, mister," I told him as he handed me back my penny.

I walked briskly back to the car and got in, telling Richie to be careful not to peel out when he took off. I watched the store clerk through the window to see if he was writing down our license plate number as Richie pulled away, but he wasn't. He had his nose back in his book.

Must be a good book, I thought.

I finally allowed myself to relax a little bit when Richie maneuvered the on-ramp heading south on 91. I cranked up the music on Cherry's stereo, and we rolled down the windows, relishing the feel of the wind blowing through our hair. Richie and I were free! I eased the seat back, took my shoes off, and put my feet up on the dashboard, something Richie told me that Jim would've killed me for. We had ourselves a giddy bout of laughter about that.

At one point on the highway, we were driving next to a middle-aged guy in a yellow Corvette. His windows were also down, and he could hear our music blasting. He did a double take at Richie driving and then shrugged. He raised up the devil horns and then passed us. Richie and I looked at each other and then burst out laughing.

That was when I discovered how fascinating it was to look into other people's cars as we passed them. For instance, a man dressed in a suit and dark sunglasses driving a silver Mercedes had his fist raised while he was singing passionately. His windows were up, so I couldn't hear what he was listening to, but the sight was hilarious. In a green station wagon, a mother was furiously yelling at her kids in the backseat, quickly glancing between them and the road. The kids were fighting amongst themselves, not listening to a word she was saying.

A sleazy-looking man in a blue BMW was tightly gripping his steering wheel, his head leaning back against his headrest. His eyes were almost closed, but his mouth was open. I was trying to figure out what was wrong with him. He looked like he was in pain or something. As I was looking at him, he noticed me and laughed. Then, a woman popped her head up from his lap and looked at me, wiping her finger along her lip. I felt my cheeks getting hot as I blushed and looked away. From the corner of my eye, I could see them both still laughing.

Down the road from them, we came upon a young woman with pink hair in a Volkswagen Rabbit. She was driving alone and heavily crying. She had dark blue mascara streaks running down her cheeks. As she absently wiped at her eyes, I saw that her fingernails were painted black. She looked so deeply sad that I felt bad for her.

Then, Richie shouted, "Holy shit, this woman has her tits out over there!"

"Where?" I asked, quickly turning my head. But there was no woman and definitely no tits.

"Made you look," he said, guffawing at my expense.

"Fucker."

"You fuck her. You brought her to the party."

"Asshole."

"It's better to be an asshole than a whole ass like you are."

"Shit head."

"Hmm, I don't have one for that," he mumbled. "But I have this." He deliberately lifted up his ass cheek and let out a rumbling fart. It distinctly sounded like his ass said the word *broink*. We howled with laughter and slapped each other five for good measure.

Luckily, the windows were already down.

Then Danzig came on the radio, and Richie told me to crank it up. It was time to rock out again, this time to the evil serenade of Glenn Danzig's smooth crooning. I switched back and forth between air guitar and air drums for a while as we sang along, but I was soon looking out my window again, losing myself in the music, wondering what other interesting things I would see in the other cars.

It took us another hour to cut down through the middle of Massachusetts and cross into Connecticut. My stomach growled with hunger as we saw signs for Hartford and New Haven. When I looked at my highlighted route on the map, I saw that we would later get off of Highway 91 and merge onto 95 South in New Haven. We decided that that would be a great place to stop and have lunch.

Unfortunately, lunch ended up costing us a lot more than it should have.

* * *

We made it to New Haven at around one o'clock in the afternoon. Richie took Exit 3 off of Highway 91 and decided it would be prudent to switch license plates again. We found a parking garage this time and switched license plates with a beat-up old Jeep Cherokee. Our stomachs couldn't wait much longer, so we decided on fast food. After a brief debate on which food chain was best, we decided to go to whichever one we saw first, which turned out to be a Burger King. When we got there, Richie parked in the back by the dumpster.

"You never know, man," Richie said. "The owner of that Jeep we lifted the plates off of could come to Burger King for a bite, since it's not too far away from the parking garage. And with Cherry parked out front, it would be just our luck that he strolls by and recognizes his own plates. It's a small chance, I know. But it's not one I want to take."

Good enough for me, I thought. I was impressed but also a little startled with Richie's forethought.

The line inside Burger King proved to be quite long. Just as we got to the back of the line and stood there, a pair of rough-looking guys in their mid-twenties came in and stood behind us. One of them was very tall and muscular, with a blond brush cut and icy blue eyes. He had a goatee and a gold feather earring hanging from his left ear. His blue jeans were full of holes, and he donned a black T-shirt with Jake "The Snake" Roberts on it. The other guy was shorter and stockier, with a swarthy complexion and dark eyes. He had a shaved head and a goatee, and he wore a nose ring. His jeans were black, and his T-shirt warned, "When I snap, you'll be the first one to go." Both of them had tattoos covering their arms, too.

I avoided eye contact with them and saw that Richie was doing the same. They were loudly engaged in conversation, debating about who was more of a badass, Steven Seagal or Jean-Claude Van Damme. When we made it to the counter, we placed our order "for here" instead of taking it "to go," because we wanted to sit down in a booth and relax for a while before we headed back out.

Richie reached into his pocket to pull out a twenty dollar bill to pay for the food, and the whole bundle came out with it, falling onto the floor. We scrambled around to quickly pick it up, not wanting anyone to see how much money we were carrying. I looked up and saw one of the guys behind us quickly look away from me. When the bundle of money was safely back in Richie's pocket, I spared another look at the two guys behind us. They had resumed their conversation and appeared disinterested in us, so I thought we were fine.

When our order was ready, we sat in a booth by the exit. We wolfed down our food wordlessly, half-listening to a Bruce Hornsby song that was piping through the dining room. We were famished, because neither of us had eaten breakfast that morning. The two ruffians who were behind us in line were now sitting diagonally from us in another booth. I spied them from the corner of my eye and saw that they were hunched over a pair of drinks, speaking quietly. I found it peculiar, considering how loud they were conversing earlier.

"Did you know that some girls' vaginas go sideways?" Richie asked, his mouth full of french fries.

I laughed and choked on the sip of Coke that I had just taken. Richie loved to do that to me—make me laugh when I was drinking something.

"What the hell are you talking about?" I asked, still laughing.

"It's mostly Asian women with sideways vaginas, but sometimes you'll find other girls with the same affliction."

I laughed even harder at this. The funniest part for me was that Richie somehow maintained a straight face. He looked at me as if he were telling me something factual like the sky was blue or that birds migrated south for the winter. Of course, having never seen a vagina at that point in my life, I couldn't be entirely sure that it *wasn't* a fact.

"You're just bullshitting me," I managed to say between chuckles.

"They can't go down slides in crowded parks, either," he said, ignoring what I had just said to him.

"Why not?"

"Because if they do, everyone else in the park will hear this." He brought his index finger up to his lips and moved it up and down over them while he let his voice out in a monotone way, which made a sort of bubbling sound. If I had been taking another sip of Coke just then, Richie would have been wearing it, because I burst out laughing.

He smiled wide and sat back, evidently very proud of himself.

I looked over at the two guys and saw the one with the brush cut looking at me. I quickly looked away, wondering why they were still here when all they had were drinks. I passed it off as paranoia, remembering the store clerk back in Massachusetts. I had been paranoid that *he* was suspicious of me, too, but that had turned out to be unfounded.

"So, we're gonna hop back onto 91 and then take 95 south after that," Richie said. He took the highlighted atlas from out of his pocket. "That will take us through New York. Hey, maybe we can drive by the jail and wave to my father."

85

"Would you want to stop and visit him?" I asked.

"As cool as that sounds, I don't think it would be very smart," he explained. "I'm sure they wouldn't have pictures of me down in New York, but you never know. My mom might think to tell the cops that I might go there, so they could be waiting for me."

"Yeah, I guess you're right. We should get going soon, don't you think?"

"Who died and made you the boss?"

"Bruce Springsteen and Tony Danza," I retorted, thinking I was clever.

Richie thought about it for a second and then gave me a token giggle. I loved him for that. Although I personally never felt that I was even close to being as funny as Richie, he never once made me feel otherwise. We emptied our trays in the trash and walked out of the building. I was peripherally aware that the two guys had also gotten up, but I didn't really think anything of it. I had decided to stop being so paranoid.

As we headed out behind the Burger King, I noticed too late that the two ruffians were following us. Just as I started to tell Richie, one of them called out to us. Richie seemed not to notice. He was still talking about whether or not he would have sex with Jodie Foster if he could. The hairs on the back of my neck stood up. We were still about ten feet away from the car. Could we get to the car, get in, and take off before they caught up to us? I didn't think so. The voice behind us spoke again, this time closer.

"Hey, can you kids give us directions to the mall?"

I turned in time to see that it was the brush-cut guy. I looked at Richie, whose eyes narrowed with mistrust as he stopped and turned around. I immediately understood that we should not have stopped, because it gave them a chance to catch up to us.

"Oh, we're not from Connecticut," Richie said.

"You're not? Isn't that your car over there?" the brush-cut guy asked, pointing to Cherry. "It has Connecticut plates."

They were at arm's length to us now. The bald guy said nothing as he glared at us, effectively scaring the shit out of me.

"We're visiting someone here, and we're borrowing their car,"

I stammered. A faint touch of smile appeared at the corners of the bald guy's mouth. He knew I was lying. I also noticed that he had one hand in his pocket. I felt panic start to creep into me. I wanted to run, but Richie wasn't budging. *Can't we just run to an area with more people?* I thought. I wished I could have telepathically communicated this with Richie.

"Is that so?" Brush-cut asked. "How old are you kids? You don't even look old enough to shave, let alone drive a car."

"Listen … we don't want any trouble with you guys. We were just leaving," Richie announced.

"Not until you give us that wad of cash that you have," the bald guy finally spoke. His voice was so deep it sounded almost fake, like a Hollywood movie effect.

"We don't have any—"

"Don't fuckin' lie to us," Brush-cut warned. "I saw it fall on the floor. I saw at *least* a couple of hundred dollar bills in that wad."

My heart sank. There was no way out of this.

"I'm not giving you anything. Just leave us alone," Richie insisted. "Let's go, Shelly."

As Richie turned toward the car, the bald guy pulled his hand out of his pocket and pulled out a knife. The blade looked about three inches long and extremely sharp.

"Oh, I think you'll give us the money," the bald guy reassured.

My legs felt as if they would give out at any second. My heart felt like it had been evicted from my chest and relocated to my throat. I couldn't believe this was happening. I glimpsed at Richie and noticed something strange. He kept glancing over his shoulder at Cherry, as if there were something in there he desperately needed.

"What are you lookin' at boy?" the bald guy asked. "Don't even think about making a run for it. I'll gut you like a fish."

Richie leveled his gaze at the two ruffians, and I could tell that he wanted to resist them, to tackle them. Seeing the fear written on my face must have changed things for him, though, because he soon resigned himself to defeat. Sighing, he reached into his pocket and pulled out the bundle of cash that he had taken from Jim's wallet. He handed it to Brush-cut without a word. A clear hatred burned in Richie's eyes. Brush-cut fanned through the money, estimating the amount. Apparently satisfied, he raised his eyebrows and whistled.

"Thanks, boys," Brush-cut grinned. "Nice doing business with you. Wrong place, wrong time for you. *Right* place, *right* time for us." He slapped the bald guy's chest and told him, "Let's go." Then they jogged away without further word or interaction. Richie glared at them as they disappeared around the corner.

* * *

Neither of us said anything until we were back on the highway. Not even one full day on the road, and we had gotten mugged. I just couldn't believe it. Hoping for a miracle, I searched through Cherry's glove compartment to see if there was anything of value enclosed. I found napkins, ketchup packets, bottle caps, two pens, a notebook with nothing but doodles of Andy Capp and women's breasts, an IROC-Z owner's manual, assorted insurance documents, the registration, and a folded New Hampshire road map. As Richie took the exit for 95 south, he began shaking his head in disbelief. He was fuming.

"Fuck, fuck … *fuck!*" he roared, hitting the steering wheel with each word. I had been zoning out, watching the buildings go by from the window, and I was startled by his outburst. "What the fuck are we gonna do?"

"We still have the money that I took from my closet stash," I reasoned. "And at least we're still alive. They left us alone after they took the money."

"How much do we have left?"

I pulled out a much smaller bundle of cash, counted it, and then shoved it back into my pocket. We were screwed.

"Seventy-seven dollars," I muttered.

"That's it? That's not even enough money for gas for the rest of the way, let alone food and drinks. We're fucked, Shelly." He said in a panicky voice. Whenever he was upset about something, his New York accent was more apparent.

"Fucked by the fickle finger of fate," I agreed, trying to be funny and failing. Richie just continued to shake his head and curse under his breath.

Silence fell over us again as we contemplated our situation. I gazed out of the window once more, observing the carcasses of blown-out tires strewn along the sides of the highway. There was just too much to think about. What would we do once we ran out of money? Would we still be able to go to Mexico? Would we have to turn back?

"It's not your fault," I said.

"Yes, it is, Shelly. I could have done something about it if I wasn't so stupid."

"What are you talking about? What the hell could you have done?"

Richie sighed and said, "Well, don't freak out, okay?"

"Freak out about what?"

"I don't know why I didn't tell you before, but … I took Jim's gun," he admitted. "It's in my duffel bag."

"Oh, Jesus, Richie."

"I know," he blurted. "I should have told you, but I didn't know what you would say."

"I can't believe this. A gun? What if it goes off or something? Do you even know how to use a gun?"

"Don't worry, man. A few times, when Jim was having good days, he would let me fire off some shots at his spent beer cans out behind the house. I know how to handle it."

"I sure hope so."

"You worry too much, Shit head."

"And you masturbate too much," I quipped.

"I checked the clip, and there are only three bullets in it. But I think it's still good to have it, man. If I would have been carrying it earlier instead of forgetting it in my bag, we'd still have our money."

I shook my head, still floored that he had a gun. My parents didn't believe in guns, so I had never seen one in real life. I recalled overhearing a gun argument a couple of years ago between my father and my uncle. My uncle had said, "Guns don't kill people. *People* kill people." My father had argued that guns enable people to kill people. I didn't have a stance on guns at the time, but I remembered how cool Bruce Willis looked with one in the movie *Die Hard*. I eyed Richie's duffel bag in the backseat.

"Can I see it?" I asked.

Richie furrowed his brow at me. "It's not a toy, you know."

"I know. I just wanna see it."

"Fine," he said. Keeping one hand on the steering wheel, he reached back and grabbed the duffel bag and put it on my lap. "Just be careful, man. Have you ever handled a gun?"

I told him no, and he said to keep my finger away from the trigger as I fished around in the bag. After a couple of seconds, I finally felt the touch of cold steel. I put my hand around the grip of the gun and lifted it up to my face to look at it.

"Fuck man, keep it down! If someone sees that, they'll call the cops. And don't point the fucking gun at me. Point it at the floor! Christ, Shelly."

I lowered the gun and looked around sheepishly. Luckily, there were no cars beside us at the moment. I was surprised at how light the gun was, considering how much damage it could do. It felt like it was only a couple of pounds. I noticed the Beretta logo on the grip, three arrows and three circles above the words "P. Beretta." Along the side of the gun, it read, "Pietro Beretta Gardone V.T. Mod. 92FS." When I was finished looking at it, Richie told me to hand it to him. He wanted to carry it on him from now on in case we ran into any more trouble. He stuffed it in the back of his pants and concealed it with his shirt.

"Sometimes when I was home alone, I used to pull it out of Jim's sock drawer and just hold it in my hands," Richie said. "I always imagined myself going in their room at night and shooting Jim in the face with it."

"I don't like it," I admitted.

Richie just shrugged and continued driving.

When we drove through New York, I thought he might say something about his father, but he remained uncommunicative. I began observing the other drivers on the highway again. I started creating back stories for each of them in my head to kill time and to take my mind off of what had happened.

The grumpy old man clutching the steering wheel in the pickup truck had "just lost his job and was trying to figure out how to tell his wife when he got home." The black girl talking on her car phone "was calling her mother to tell her that she was pregnant and she planned on marrying the father, even if she didn't get her mother's blessing." The balding guy picking his nose in the Monte Carlo "was a chronic masturbator who wore women's panties and lipstick at night."

By the time we crossed into New Jersey, Richie had come around a little bit. He commented on the Skid Row song that was playing, telling me that he thought they were from New Jersey. We talked a little after that about anything but money.

By the time night had fallen, we had made it to Pennsylvania. We stopped in a little burg called Allentown to fill up on gas, switch license plates, and eat. At McDonald's, we talked off and on while we stirred our straws around our Cokes, but mostly, we were quiet. Needless to say, we were very watchful of those around us.

Back in the car, I felt sleepy. We had driven through five states already, and until that point, I had never been outside of New Hampshire. As Richie drove in silence, my thoughts wandered to my parents back in Overture. I wondered what they would do when they read my note and found out I had run away. I hadn't told Richie about the note I had written. I didn't want him to know. I didn't know if he would make fun of me, but it just seemed that it was something personal between me and my parents.

The volume of the radio was turned low in the car, because neither of us felt like rocking out anymore. I could hear the droning of Cherry's wheels on the pavement, obeying their new master's whim, carrying us gently down the highway. In my train of thought, my parents departed, and Tiffany boarded. Sweet, beautiful Tiffany. I traced the outline of her note in my back pocket. Smiling, I fell asleep and dreamed of her.

Chapter 8
THE DINER

October 2008

Sitting at Pippy's Diner, I sipped my coffee and watched the gloomy waitress work the tables. When she came back to take my order, I asked her when they changed the name of the diner, and she just shrugged and ambled back to the kitchen. I found myself wondering if anyone in this town was friendly anymore. I was beginning to miss Cleveland.

The Midwest was a great place to live, but I had been looking forward to the salt-of-the-earth New Englanders. I expected to feel some sort of camaraderie when I got here, but I was an outsider now. *So much for that,* I thought. *It's just as well anyway. Ohio is my home now, and after my visit with Richie, I'll be going back.*

My apartment in Cleveland sat on the west side of the Cuyahoga River on the outskirts of a nice neighborhood called Edgewater. Our biggest claims to fame in Edgewater were the two summer festivals we hosted. The Clifton Arts & Musicfest took place on Clifton Boulevard, and the Festival of Freedom was a Fourth of July event in Edgewater State Park. Personally, I thought the best part of Edgewater was a lakefront restaurant called Don's Lighthouse. I took my girlfriend there for our first date.

"Where you from?" The waitress asked when she brought

my food. I was surprised with her change in demeanor. Then I remembered that New Hampshire folk could sometimes be standoffish to visitors at first. Once they had a minute to size you up, they could be very friendly.

"Uh, well, I'm originally from here," I said. "But now I live in Cleveland."

A big smirk spread across her face, accentuating her dimples. "Cleveland, huh? The Sox kicked your ass in every single game this year."

I smiled back at her. I had forgotten just how serious the people in New England were about their baseball. They even had a term for it: Red Sox Fever. "I haven't really followed baseball since I was a kid, but I *do* know that the Sox didn't make it to the World Series this year *either*, so you should come down off of your high horse."

She laughed, and it made her look beautiful. I got the feeling that she hadn't had much to smile about lately. I pondered what was going on her life but decided it best not to pry.

"Are you from around here?" I asked.

"Yeah, I was born down in ManchVegas," she said. ManchVegas was a nickname for a city in Southern New Hampshire called Manchester. "Moved up here two years ago. Hold on a minute."

She grabbed a pot of coffee and walked away to make her rounds with the other customers. As I ate my food, I looked around the restaurant. It hadn't changed since I was last here. The motif was typical of a diner, and 1950s memorabilia was strewn about on the walls. There was an old-fashioned jukebox in the corner, currently playing Fats Domino. The floor consisted of black-and-white checkered tiles, and the red leather-topped stools were chrome, matching the exterior of the place.

The cook put a plate of blueberry pancakes up in the order window, and the sweet smell wafted over to me. It brought me back to my tenth birthday. My parents had brought John and me to the diner, because their blueberry pancakes were my favorite. After we found a table, John and I sauntered over to the jukebox as usual.

We made our selections and coaxed the coins from our parents, and then we sat down to order. All four of us asked for blueberry pancakes. After we started eating, my favorite selection, "Surfin' Bird" by The Trashmen came on and immediately started to skip. I quickly shot up out of my seat to go hit the jukebox, but I accidentally knocked my plate of pancakes on the floor with my elbow.

I stopped and looked down at the mangled pancakes and began to cry. It was my birthday, my favorite oldies song was skipping, and I had just knocked my favorite food on the floor. Things couldn't get much worse in the eyes of a ten-year-old.

Then, John went over to the jukebox to knock it back on track and my father asked for a spare plate from the waitress. After the new plate arrived, my mother forked a couple of pancakes from everyone's plates onto it. I was once again enjoying my scrumptious pancakes just as The Trashmen began my favorite "Papa-Oom-Mow-Mow" part. My birthday disaster was fixed. My family had saved the day.

That memory always made me smile.

I watched as the waitress finished her rounds and replaced the coffee pot on the warmer. She took my now empty plate and brought it to the kitchen. When she came back, she leaned over the counter on her elbows to talk with me again.

"So what brings you to New Hampshire again?"

"An old friend," I answered. I didn't want to get into the specifics with her. "What brought you from Manchester to Overture?"

"The promise of fame and fortune," she said with a straight face.

I erupted in loud and unexpected laughter, causing people in the diner to look over at us. The waitress chuckled, clearly pleased with herself.

"You're kind of cute when you laugh," she said. "What's your name anyway?"

I felt my face getting hot then. "Uh, thanks ... I'm Shelton. How about you?"

"I'm Jamie. It's nice to meet you." She extended her hand for me to shake, and her sleeve came up a little, revealing a mesh of cuts on her arm. Some were a faded pink, while others looked fairly fresh. She noticed me looking and quickly pulled her hand back, tugging at her sleeve. A few seconds of awkward silence passed, and then she spoke.

"Gay baby," she said.

"Excuse me?"

"Gay baby … haven't you ever heard that?"

"Honestly?" I said. "I have no idea what you're talking about."

"Some people say that every time there is an awkward silence, a gay baby is born."

"Isn't that a bit offensive?"

"It's just a joke, jeez. Lighten up, Cleveland."

A man who was sitting farther down the counter from me called her over, and she immediately went to him. The bell over the diner's door rang, and I looked to see an old couple entering. The man held the door for the woman, and when they got to a table, he pulled her chair out for her. *Who says chivalry is dead?* I thought with a smile.

The entrance bell rang again, and this time a burly woman with a pronounced limp walked in. As she went by, I observed a dolphin tattoo on her ankle, and it gave me goose bumps. It made me think of my recurring dream—the train tracks, the lake, the tattoo with the dolphins and the turtle. I shook my head to clear the images from my mind.

"Got fleas or something?" Jamie asked, now finished with the other customer.

"Huh? No, just clearing my head," I said.

"So anyway," she said. She leaned back on the counter behind her and pushed her chest out a little. She was also fiddling with her tongue piercing again. "How about it?"

"How about what?"

"I get off work in a couple hours. You gonna be around for a while? You could come pick me up."

I was stunned. I felt my face getting red again. She trained her eyes on me, waiting for an answer. As flattered as I was, I knew I couldn't. Even though we were at odds lately, I had a girlfriend back home. Besides that, this girl was obviously troubled. She was a mess and who knew what else. I didn't want to contribute to that in any way with a meaningless one-night stand.

"Uh, I have a girlfriend. I'm sorry," I said. She moved away from the counter and narrowed her eyes at me. "But listen, you don't need to do stuff like that anyway. You should value yourself more than that. You're an attractive girl, and I liked you even before your proposition."

"Don't be psychoanalyzing *me*. You don't even know me. What's your problem?"

"I didn't mean to—"

"You think you're too good for me or something?"

"No," I said.

"I thought you seemed like a nice guy, but I was way off. I think you should just leave."

"Jamie—"

"Are you ready for your check now?" she asked.

"Yeah, sure. But please, I really didn't—"

"Thank you, and have a nice day, sir," she said and then slapped the check down on the counter and walked away.

Confounded, I took out my wallet to pay the bill. I thought about giving her a fifty percent tip out of guilt and then thought better of it. I didn't do anything wrong. After I laid the money on the counter, I got up to leave. I decided against any further interaction with the people of Overture. I would go see Richie and then get the fuck out of here.

On my way out, I noticed a bulletin board by the door. Amidst all of the business cards and flyers, a missing child poster caught my eye. The girl looked to be about fourteen years old. Every time I saw things like that, I got a chill. *Back in 1991, I was on one of those posters.* I wondered if the girl was kidnapped or if she was a runaway, if she was alone and scared or in any type of danger. I had to look away.

Inevitably, I was reminded of myself and Richie. I thought about that conversation we had on the highway about Richie's fatal confrontation with Jim. I wished that he would have told me the whole story. I understood why he didn't, but things may have turned out differently if I would have known all of the details.

Things might not have gotten so out of hand.

Chapter 9
BROTHERHOOD

September 1991

When I woke up, it was still dark. Cherry's dashboard clock read 2:13 AM. My neck was stiff, and I felt cold. As I turned the heat on in the car, I looked over at Richie. He was wide-eyed, apparently concentrating on the road, both hands on the wheel. In that moment, I felt closer to him than I ever had. I looked at his face and thought that I could see a glimpse of the man he would become. He may have killed someone, but that didn't change that fact that I was proud to be his friend.

Still groggy, I shifted in my seat and closed my eyes, thinking back to when I had first met him. He had been telling anyone who would listen that his father was Dino Gallo, the incarcerated mobster down in New York. Being impressed and a little scared, I chanced talking to him. I approached him one day in the cafeteria and asked him question after question about what it was like being the son of a mobster. He seemed pleased to have a sounding board, and I was just ecstatic that I had found someone to talk to.

When I had asked him if he ever visited his father, he shrugged and told me that his father may as well be dead, because he'd never see him again. I told him that dying was not the same thing as not being able to visit with a living person. In true Richie fashion, he teased me, saying, "Who made *you* the authority on death?"

After I told him about John's death, he clammed up for a moment and then started asking me questions about it. We formed an unspoken bond of suffering that day, united by the shit we had both endured.

I was ripped out of my thoughts by the sound of a blaring horn. I looked up in time to see that we were headed straight for the guardrail on the side of the highway. Richie had fallen asleep driving. I reached across and yanked on the wheel, pulling us back into our lane just before impact. Richie woke up and confusedly looked around as the car that had beeped its horn drove by. The driver peered in at us and shook his head.

"Jesus Christ," I yelled. "You almost killed us!"

"I must have fallen asleep."

"Yeah, and if it wasn't for that guy beeping his horn, we would be laying on the side of the road right now," I said. My pulse was already slowing, but I still felt shaky.

"Take a chill pill, man. We're fine now," Richie said.

I took a deep breath and looked around. Because I saw nothing but trees, pavement, and darkness outside of the window, I didn't even know where the hell we were. I had fallen asleep in Pennsylvania hours ago, so we could be anywhere.

"All right, I'm sorry for yelling," I said. "But we have to stop somewhere and get some sleep. You've been driving all day and night, dude."

Richie agreed and told me that he would take the next exit and find somewhere to pull over. We passed a sign that said we were on Highway 81, followed by an exit sign that read Martinsburg. Richie took the exit, and I checked the map, discovering that we were now in West Virginia. There was a commuter parking lot just off the exit, and Richie pulled in, parking in the first empty spot.

"I'm sorry, Shelly," Richie said after he killed the engine.

"Don't worry about it, man. I just wish we could have gotten that guy's license plate so we could track him down and mail him a thank you card," I joked.

"I'm not talking about that. I'm talking about this whole mess, taking you with me on the run. I'm not sorry I killed Jim, but I could have just kept driving. I didn't need to mix you up in all of this. I fucked up, man."

"You didn't twist my arm," I consoled, noticing that he had begun to cry.

"No, but you don't deserve *this*," he said. "When I was on my way over to the Backyard to get you, I … I thought I had this all figured out. It was the *perfect* plan. We would have *just* enough money to get down to Mexico, and then we could get jobs somewhere. I figured once we started working, we could even save up enough to start that music store we always used to talk about, you know? And I knew that things were going bad for you at home, too. So I thought it would be great for us to get away, you know? I thought that everything would be okay for us.

"But then those *assholes* in Connecticut stole our fucking money. *Now* look at us. We only have enough money for breakfast tomorrow morning, and then we're finished. No more money—zilch, zip, nada. And look at this. We have less than a half a tank of gas left. Once we run out, that's it. The jig is up."

"Take a breath, man," I said. "There must be something we can do."

"Oh, yeah? Like what?"

"I don't know. Maybe we could sell the car."

"Who would we sell it to, dude? Think about it. Are we just gonna walk into a car dealership with a stolen car?"

After careful consideration, I answered, "We could sell it to like a junkyard or something, couldn't we?"

"Come on, Shelly. Do you see a junkyard around here? Plus, I don't think it's a good idea to try to sell a stolen car anyway. What if the people we try to sell it to rat us out?"

"I'm just trying to think," I said. I thought about telling Richie that we could rob a store with the gun, but I decided against it. I didn't want to get us into even deeper trouble. Besides, I think I would have felt terrible doing something like that.

Richie looked out the window and lit a cigarette. Tears formed in his eyes again.

"I just ... I just keep asking myself why. Why did I have to drop that wad of bills on the floor? Why didn't I just keep the money in one of our bags? Why didn't I even notice those guys? Why wasn't I carrying the gun? Why? Why? Why? I don't know. I just ... don't *know*."

He took a long drag off of his cigarette and continued, "I guess it's because I'm a fuckup. *That's* why I said I'm sorry earlier, Shelly. I'm sorry because I'm a fuckup. It's fine if *my* life is going to hell, because I'm just a piece of shit, but I shouldn't have dragged you down with me."

"Don't say stuff like that, Richie. You're not a piece of shit."

"But you're a *good* person, Shelly. You shouldn't be in this mess. It was so fucking selfish of me to bring you along. You know, even when your parents got divorced, that wouldn't have been the end for you. You still had a chance to live *somewhat* of a normal life, right? I shouldn't have— I just ... I just shouldn't have. I hate myself, Shelly, and I deserve to fucking die."

He squeezed his eyes shut and rubbed his arm over his face, roughly wiping his tears away in frustration.

"Don't talk like that," I pleaded. "You didn't fuck anything up, and you definitely don't deserve to *die*. How could you have known that shit would happen the way it did?" I put my hand on his arm. "Nothing is your fault. Like I said, you didn't twist my arm. My life sucked, too, in case you don't remember. My parents could be jumping for joy right now for all I know. None of this is your fault, none of it."

Richie shrugged.

"I *chose* to go with you, Richie. And no matter what happens, I'm glad that I did. You know, when John died, I felt like I wanted to die, too. But then you moved to Overture, and I had a brother again, man. You're my *brother*, and I'll go with you *anywhere*."

Tears began falling from my own eyes, but I didn't try to stop them. There was no reason for shame. We were brothers. We looked at each other for a minute, crying like fucking babies and not hiding it. We formed an even closer bond just then.

Richie cleared his throat and said with a sniffle, "Do you really mean it, Shelly? Do you really think of me as a brother?"

100

"Yes, I mean it. You're my only family from now on. Well, Cherry, too," I grinned, trying to lighten the mood.

Richie smiled at me, looking rather chuffed. I could tell he was thinking about something, his head cocked slightly, his eyes looking past me. Just as I was about to ask him what he was thinking about, he finally said, "Do you remember in history class when we were learning about John Adams, and Mrs. Harelip sent us to the principal's office for laughing so hard?"

I nodded, remembering it well. It had happened soon after Richie and I had become friends, just before summer vacation. Our history teacher, Mrs. Harris, who seemed obsessed with John Adams, had an ever-so-slight cleft lip and talked with a not-so-slight lisp. Behind her back, everyone called her Mrs. Harelip.

We had been learning about young John Adams, and she had been reading us excerpts from his diary. She had read one particular entry written in February 1763, where he discussed the Caucus Club. Richie and I had looked at each other and burst out in stifled giggles at the word "caucus."

"Excuse me, Mrs. Harris?" Richie had interrupted, barely containing his laughter. "Shelton here was clearing his throat, and I didn't hear the line you just read."

Mrs. Harris shot me an annoyed glance, and I lowered my head, holding my breath to force back the laughter. She obliged Richie, reading the line over again. "Please pay attention, class. 'This day learned that the Caucus Club meets, at certain times, in the Garret of Tom Dawes.'"

"What does *cock*-is mean?" Richie asked, once again interrupting her. He emphasized the first syllable of the word with a huge grin. He was trying to get her to say the word as many times as he could. It was funny to hear the word "caucus," but it was downright hilarious when pronounced with her lisp.

"A caucus is a meeting typically for political party members to discuss candidates or select delegates," Mrs. Harris explained patiently. She had obviously not caught on to what Richie was doing.

"So if I want to hold my own caucus someday, that would be

Tom Jarvis

okay? Or would I have to have someone else hold my caucus for me?"

I wasn't able to hold it in any longer. I cackled loudly, which set Richie off, too. Our faces were turning red as we convulsed with laughter. The entire classroom watched us, some with perplexed expressions and some with smirks. Realization then dawned on Mrs. Harris, and she became furious. She ordered us both to the principal's office, and we laughed the whole way there. Thinking of it always brought a smile to my face.

"Yes, I remember," I told Richie.

"Well, if I remember right, that was pretty much the first time me and you had a good laugh together, and it was also the first time we got in trouble together."

"Yeah, I'm pretty sure you're right, but what does that have to do with what we were just talking about?" I asked.

"I was just thinking. We don't know what's gonna happen here, especially when we run out of money. You never know. We've been lucky so far, but I could get pulled over or something. And then we would be done. I would get locked up, and you would be shipped back to Overture."

"But you're being careful, though, right? You're not speeding or anything. And we've been switching plates."

"I know. I'm just saying that anything can happen."

"What's your point?"

"Well, even if they did somehow catch us and I got sent up like my old man, I don't think that it would be forever," he said. "I think that because it was self-defense or whatever, I might get a smaller sentence. I wouldn't be in there for life. Even my _father_ didn't get life in prison, so I don't think _I_ would."

"Are you saying you want to go back and turn yourself in?"

"Fuck no, man. I think I would rather die than go to prison or juvie. God knows what happens in places like that," he said with a touch of panic. "Just forget about that, okay? What I'm saying is that if something like that happens, would you still be my friend when I got out? Would you still be my brother?" He asked, leveling his eyes at me solemnly.

"Of course I would, dude. What kind of question is that?" I snapped.

"Calm down. I just wanted to make sure. So, what I'm thinking is if we ever get separated somehow, like I get caught or something, and we somehow lose touch, let's make a pact that we will meet again someday."

"Yeah, I like that. That sounds cool. But how will we know where and when to meet?"

"Well, I don't think I would get sent up for more than fifteen years or so. So, how about when we turn thirty? We could make it on the one day when we are the same age, your birthday. And we'll make it in Overture, of course. We'll get together and smoke a cigarette for old times' sake, even if one of us has quit. It will be our thirty-year caucus."

He grinned and lit a cigarette.

"I like that," I admitted. "But wait—what if one of us can't make it for some reason?"

"Okay, how about this then? We will each do everything in our power to contact the person somehow to let them know, and if we can't meet on *that* day, we'll promise to at least meet that same year."

I tried to think of any other loopholes and found none. "Sounds good, man," I said.

"Do you promise?"

"Yes, I promise."

"Me too."

Richie spat in his hand and held it out to me. I spat in my own and shook his, sealing the deal forever.

"There we have it, the thirty-year caucus. Wouldn't Mrs. Harelip be proud? We're holding our own caucus!"

I let out a sluggish giggle. My eyelids were becoming very heavy. I took another drag off of my cigarette and threw it out of the window. I told Richie that we really should get some sleep and reclined my seat. Minutes later, we were asleep, no idea of the outrageous adventure that would await us the next day.

PART FOUR
RUNNING FREE

Chapter 10
CATCHING OUT

September 1991

The bright orange fuel-warning light started blinking about an hour after we took off in the morning. Another half an hour later, Richie decided to exit from the highway so we would at least be close to a town when we ran out of gas. He took Exit 222 into Staunton, Virginia, and turned onto Route 250. About a mile and a half down that road, Cherry sputtered a couple of times. Then all of her dashboard lights came on, and the engine ceased. We coasted to a stop and sat wordlessly in the car for a moment, listening to Cherry's engine ticking as it cooled off.

"I guess it's time to walk," Richie muttered, getting out of the car.

We opened the hatch and retrieved our bags. As he slung one over his shoulder, Richie looked thoughtfully at the defunct IROC-Z. What he did next stunned me. He picked up a rock the size of a softball and hurled it at Cherry's windshield. The rock hit with a dull crackle, forming a web-like pattern around the point of impact, and then rolled off of the car and onto the road with a thud. Richie grunted, apparently pleased with himself as he surveyed the damage.

"What did you do that for?" I asked, bewildered.

"Because she's Jim's girl, and I have no use for that bitch anymore," he answered. With that, he swung around theatrically and began walking with a leisurely gait toward downtown Staunton.

"So what are we gonna do?" I asked, catching up to him. "Should we hitchhike?"

"No, I don't want to do that. Didn't you ever see that movie, *The Hitcher*?"

"Yeah, I did, but *we're* the hitchhikers, dumbass."

"It doesn't matter. It could go the other way around, too. The person who picks us up could be some psycho, too," Richie said.

"Well then, do you have any other ideas, or are we just gonna walk until *we* run out of gas, too?"

"Well, I saw some train tracks from the highway earlier, and when we got off, we crossed over some. From the highway, they looked like they were heading along this road."

"We don't have any money, man. How do you think we're going to buy train tickets? Oh … no way. Are you thinking that we're gonna hop a train like in the old Westerns?"

Richie nodded with a grin.

"You can't do that shit nowadays! I'm not even sure if they did that for real in *those* days," I said.

"That's *exactly* what we're gonna do, my friend. I'm sure this road or another road up ahead crosses those tracks at some point, and when they do, we're gonna follow them until we find a good place to jump on," he said.

"How the hell are we going to do that? The guys in the movies jumped on trains from their *horses*." I looked at the land around us to make my point. "And we don't have any horses, gringo."

He stopped and looked at me, holding his arms out with his palms up. "What other choice do we have, Shelly? What other choice do we have?"

"I guess you're right," I acknowledged after I had thought about it for a second.

Richie lit a cigarette and continued walking, so I followed along. I wasn't sure if we would be able to pull something like that off. Jumping onto a moving train, when I really thought about it, seemed very dangerous. The thought excited me just as much as it made me nervous, though. A memory came to me of sitting on the couch next to my father and John, eating chocolate éclairs and watching *How the West Was Won*.

The road split up ahead, and we headed toward the right onto a street called Greenville Avenue. In the distance, we saw two things that piqued our interest: a railroad overpass and a giant watering can.

As we shuffled toward the overpass, we observed that the giant watering can was an iron sculpture approximately eighteen feet high. There was a flower garden in front of it and a sign that stated that the statue had been built, "In honor of Barbara Hunter Grant." The watering can was angled forward to give the appearance of watering the garden below. Richie barely seemed to notice. He moved past the sculpture and then scrambled up the embankment and onto the train tracks. As I stood on the tracks, I looked toward the horizon. I could see what looked like a storm cloud off in the distance.

The sight gave me an unexpected shiver.

We followed the tracks for a couple of hours. They led straight through downtown Staunton to what they called the "Wharf section" of town, according to the signs. I found this to be odd, as I didn't see any water anywhere. We passed by a train station that had been converted into two restaurants, The Pullman and The Depot Grille. After another railroad overpass, we found a dead cat beside the tracks. Although this cat was a different color, it reminded me of the vagrant tabby that had come up to me a couple of days earlier in the Backyard. I wondered to myself if he ever found what he was looking for.

Finally, a short distance after the train station, we found an area that was wooded and would provide cover for us while we waited for the next train to come. We stepped off the tracks and waited there, eating the granola bars and drinking the Mountain Dews that we had bought with our last couple of dollars. As we waited, I noticed a faded symbol that looked like it had been drawn onto the side of the track with chalk. Upon closer inspection, we saw that it was a crude drawing of a train car.

"What do you suppose that means?" I asked Richie.

He shrugged, and then a raspy voice spoke up from behind us, making me jump.

"Means this here's a good place to catch out," the voice answered.

We spun around to see the owner of the voice. It was a skinny, potbellied man of about sixty years. He was wearing a herringbone flat cap that didn't quite match his outfit, which was a pair of worn-out, camouflage cargo pants and a blue sweater with holes. His gray-bearded face was wind-burnt and bore crow's feet around cloudy green eyes. Slung around his shoulder was an army green rucksack that looked like it had seen better days. He threw his head back and laughed heartily.

"Oh, did y'all think I was a bull?" he asked. He spoke in a southern drawl, and he had a jovial tone to go along with his scratchy voice.

"A what? Who … who are you? What do you want?" Richie asked with a faint tremble in his voice. He reached behind his back and gripped the gun. "We don't have any more money."

"My friends call me Dusty Rails, but y'all can just call me Dusty if that's yer preference. Now, I ain't here to steal from nobody. I'm blowed in the glass, so dontcha worry. No sirree, Bob. I'm here to catch out just like y'all." He extended his calloused hand to us in greeting.

Richie and I just looked at it, untrusting.

"Okay, okay," he said, withdrawing his hand and indifferently averting his eyes to the train tracks. "Just tryin' to be neighborly is all."

"Were you following us?" Richie asked suspiciously. His face had gone pale, and his eyes darted around nervously as he backed away from the man. I followed suit and stepped back.

"Not at first. I saw y'all Angellinas a little ways back and kept my distance, 'cause I wasn't sure what y'all were up to. Then I heard one of you mention train hoppin', and y'all just so happened to stop right at the place I was goin'," he explained, pointing at the chalked train symbol drawn on the track. "So, I decided to introduce myself since y'all seem to be fellow 'boes. Or maybe you just want to be?"

Richie and I looked at each other. I could tell that Richie, like me, didn't really understand all of what the guy was saying, but I saw his grip on the gun loosen a little now that there was more distance between us and the strange man. That eased my own tension a bit, because if Richie could relax, then I could, too. Then I remembered how Richie had completely overlooked the two ruffians in New Haven, and I tensed up again.

"What do you mean by 'boes? And why did you call us ... Angellinas? What the hell is that?" Richie demanded.

"And you said you're blowed in the glass. What does *that* mean?" I added.

"Whoa, you boys sure do got a lot to learn," Dusty laughed. His laughter ended in a violent coughing fit, after which he spit a gob of saliva and blood on the ground. "Goddamn cigarettes are killing me. Anyway, 'boes is short for hoboes. An Angellina is a young feller who's learnin' to be a hobo, and 'blowed in the glass' means y'all can trust me, I'm honest. I don't steal unless I have to." He bellowed laughter again and then added, "Now I done told y'all my name, dontcha know it's rude to not introduce yerselves?"

"Fine. I'm Richie, and this is my brother, Shelly."

"Shelton," I corrected. "So, do you like hop trains and stuff? I thought people didn't really do that anymore."

"Yep, I reckon not too many people are out there hoboin' anymore, much less catchin' out. No sirree, Bob. Not with all the progress in the world," Dusty chuckled, holding up two fingers on each hand in quotes for the word "progress." "But there are still some of us out there. Yep, mostly it's wannabe hoboes, and then there are those who have no choice. But a good lot of us still *choose* to be hoboes."

"What is catching out?" I asked eagerly. The notion that he was a real-life hobo fascinated me. Richie threw me a glance as if to say, "You don't really buy into this shit do you?"

"Oh, y'all really *do* have a lot to learn now, don't you? Catchin' out means hoppin' a train, ridin' the rails, flippin' a freighter. Do you get it now, son?" Dusty laughed jovially and coughed again. "I do believe the *real* question is what are you kids doin' out here wantin' to ride the rails? Is the spirit of Jack Wanderlust gettin' a hold of you, makin' you wanna copy the ways of the hobo? Or are y'all in some kinda trouble?"

"Jack *who*? What the fuck language are you speaking anyway? Ah, forget it. What do you care if we're in trouble or not? What do you want from us anyway?" Richie asked harshly.

Dusty shrugged heavily and then held his hands up. "All right, boy. I just thought I could help y'all out since I been doin' this most of my life. I didn't wanna see one of you get yerself killed or becomin' some Jocker's bitch, but if y'all don't want my help, I understand. Just don't get in my way when the train comes along. Good luck to you."

He turned around and walked a couple of feet away, leaving his back to us. I watched him light a cigarette and cough, and then I turned to Richie. I widened my eyes and raised my eyebrows at him. He mouthed the question "what?" to me, his arms held out in a show of exasperation.

I leaned in close to him and whispered in his ear. "Richie, if this guy can help us out, I don't see the problem."

"Dude, we can't go around trusting people. What if he's some psychopath or some pervert? Do you really wanna take that chance?"

I thought about it for a minute. For some reason, I instinctually trusted Dusty. I couldn't explain why. It was just that he hadn't seemed like he was the type to hurt someone. He had honest eyes and a down-to-earth way about him that just didn't seem to fit into what I thought a psycho would be like. I knew that I could be wrong, but like Richie had said earlier about the train, what choice did we have?

As I looked over at Dusty, who had erupted into yet another coughing fit, I took into consideration that he was old, obviously unhealthy, and rather skinny, apart from his slight potbelly. I thought that if we ran into any trouble with him, we could easily overpower him, especially because there were two of us. Even if we couldn't, there was the gun.

Weighing it out, I felt that we could learn a lot from him if he turned out to be okay. We had no money, no food, no transportation, and nowhere to go. That pretty much described this man's whole life, and he had somehow survived. I whispered my rationale to Richie, and he shrugged, indicating that it was up to me. He didn't look very convinced, but I decided that it was time for Richie to trust my judgment for once.

"Dusty," I called out as I walked over to him. I extended my hand in friendship to him. "I would like to apologize. My brother and I have been through an awful lot since we hit the road, and we aren't quick to trust strangers."

Dusty shook my hand and said, "Well, that's smart. But you can trust me, bub. I ain't never hurt nobody, and I reckon I never will."

"Hey! Train's coming," Richie yelled.

I looked in the direction Richie was pointing and saw a shiny silver train in the distance coming around the bend. When we picked up our bags, Richie and I began to hear the train as well. I squinted my eyes to see "Amtrak" written on the front of it. Dusty had already picked up his bag, but he was heading toward the woods, not the train.

"C'mon, boys. Let's go farther into the woods away from the tracks while this train goes by, lest y'all be smacked in the head with a flyin' rock," he said.

"What? What are you talking about? The train is coming. We need to be ready to jump it," Richie argued.

"No, no, no. That there is a passenger train, boy. Ain't no place to jump. We gotta wait for a *freight* train. There will be one comin' through here in about an hour," Dusty said.

We reluctantly followed him into the woods, ducking down as the train went by. As we waited, Dusty explained to us the different types of trains to ride. He had to yell to be heard over the squealing and click-clacking of the passing train. He informed us that any self-respecting hobo preferred a boxcar, but less and less of those were being manufactured anymore. He said that the next best choices were grainers, hoppers, and gondolas. Richie and I weren't sure what those were, but we had an idea that we would find out soon enough.

Dusty went on to tell us that we had some dumb luck finding the right place to catch out. He said the best places were right outside of train stations, where the train was still moving slowly enough to jump on. In the old days, he told us, a hobo could catch out inside the train yard while the train was still stopped, but nowadays, there were too many *bulls*. Bulls, he explained, were railroad cops.

The chalk drawing we saw on the side of track turned out to be what Dusty called a hobo symbol, indicating that it was a good place to catch out. He explained that in the glory days of the hobo, different symbols were used so that they could covertly communicate with each other. Some of the hoboes still used them today, he told us. He gave us some examples of different symbols that were used. The number eight turned on its side told them that police in the area were hostile toward hoboes. A cross meant that religious talking would get you food here. A square missing its top line informed them that it was a safe place to camp, but three diagonal lines indicated that it was not. There were hundreds of different symbols, some of them having the same meaning as others, he said.

"So why do they call you Dusty Rails?" I asked as the last passenger car sped by.

"We hoboes all go by monikers," Dusty explained after another hacking fit that resulted in a wad of blood-filled spit. "Used to be in the old days, hoboes used monikers so the bulls couldn't track 'em down. Nowadays, it's more like a tradition to most than it is a necessity. We hoboes like to live in anonymity, so we use these nicknames."

He yawned, exposing a mouth full of yellowing teeth, and then continued, "I chose to call myself Dusty Rails, 'cause my real name's Dustin, so it's close enough, and I just like the sound of it. Plus, I ride the rails a lot more than most of the other hoboes I know."

"What do you do for food? Do you work anywhere?" Richie inquired.

"Someone like me kinda floats from place to place, but I always find ways to make money. I have a couple of different places I've been workin' at to support my eatin', smokin', and shittin' habits." He let out a rough laugh, which was accompanied by a cough. "I kinda like to keep movin', though. I like to have the wind in my face and the dust at my heels, as they say. Lately, though, I've been stayin' at the same place. That's where I'm headed back to now."

He patiently fielded our questions until the freight train came about an hour later just like he said it would. We asked him how he knew the train schedule, and he simply told us, "I know these rails like they were the back of my hand." When I saw the train off in the distance, billowing smoke from its stack, I began to feel nervous about jumping. I expressed my doubts to Dusty as the train approached.

"Dusty, I don't know if I can do this," I said.

"C'mon now, boy. That's not the way to be. It's not as hard as it seems. All you gotta do is choose your car, run alongside it to try to match its speed, and then grab onto the ladder and jump," Dusty explained. "Plus, not to worry, I'll see that y'all get on before I do. I'll be right behind you."

I found comfort in his words. There was something in general about Dusty that just made me feel comfortable. He seemed fatherly in a way, which was something we both so desperately needed. He had a natural warmth about him that he radiated. Richie didn't seem to share the same feelings toward him as I did, but I hoped that he would eventually come around. It seemed justified to me that we should find someone so nice and helpful after the shit we had gone through back in New Haven.

The train grew closer, and the ground started vibrating beneath me. Then the sound of its steel wheels grazing the track, the clacking of its metal parts shaking, and the chugging of its engine hit my ears like a tsunami. The conductor blew the whistle, and I almost jumped out of my skin. As the train was breezing by in front of us, my teeth were chattering. Standing so close to a moving train, even though it wasn't moving at full speed, was spine-tingling.

"*There! The yellow gondola,*" Dusty yelled over the cacophonous racket of the train. He pointed toward a bright yellow train car with the words "Union Pacific" printed on its side. The car appeared shorter than the other cars, and it sort of resembled a long box with no cover. "*Throw your bags in before you jump! Richie first, then Shelton,*" *then me! Run as fast as you can. Then grab the ladder and climb ... and for God's sake, climb fast!"*

Richie got in front of me and sprinted alongside the train. I followed suit with Dusty in tow. When the yellow gondola was beside us, Richie threw his bags in and grabbed for its ladder. He missed and almost fell on his face, but he found purchase the second time he reached out. He began climbing in midjump as if he was part of Cirque du Soleil or something, bringing his feet up to the bottom rung and continuing up. When I caught up to the ladder, I felt nauseous. Despite the cool wind rushing by, I could feel sweat racing down my back.

"Go! Go! Go!" Dusty shouted from behind me.

I threw my bags up and over into the gondola and held my breath. When I reached for the bottom rung, I grasped my hand around it securely. I was momentarily ecstatic that I hadn't miss it like Richie had, but my excitement was snuffed out like a candle, because I hesitated. The force of the train yanked me violently off of the ground. It felt like my arm had been ripped right out of its socket. Then, I felt pain searing through my right leg as it dragged along the rocks beside the track. I screamed, and little black spots began to form in the corners of my vision as I started to pass out. I held tightly onto the ladder rung and tried pulling myself up, but my arms suddenly felt weak and heavy.

"Shelly, jump! You'll be pulled under the fucking wheels!" Richie screamed.

I looked up at him, and a strange calm overcame me. I heard a voice in my head saying, "Just let go. Everything will end." Just as I was about to let go of the rung, I felt a hand grabbing the seat of my pants and pushing me up forcefully. When I snapped out of my delirium, I realized it was Dusty. He lifted me about three feet up in air, high enough for me to put my foot on the bottom rung.

"Climb, goddamn you!" Dusty roared.

I wrenched my left leg up onto the bottom rung and pushed up hard. When I swung the injured right leg up and put my weight on it, pain screamed through my head. The black spots burst into my eyes again, but this time I was able to fight them back. Despite the pain in my leg and my shoulder, I continued climbing. When I neared the top, Richie grabbed the back of my shirt and pulled me the rest of the way into the gondola. As I scrambled over the lip of the train car, he lost his balance, and we both crashed down onto the hard steel at the bottom. Falling unconscious, I took one last look up and saw Dusty coughing and wheezing as he swung his leg over the top of the gondola.

And then I passed out.

* * *

I was jerked awake by a sudden stinging pain piercing through my right leg. Something digging—what was going on? The clamorous sound of the train inside the gondola was amplified because the car was empty. The air inside smelled like rusty, wet steel. As I regained consciousness, the pain sensations grew stronger. Confused, I looked around and saw Richie and Dusty leaning over my legs. Dusty's back was to me, but I could see Richie's face, which was almost green. He appeared on the verge of throwing up. When he noticed that my eyes were open, sympathy filled his face.

"What's happening?" I croaked thinly and then yelped as I felt another sharp dig on my shin. I propped myself up on my elbows, trying to see what Dusty was doing to me.

"Hold still," Dusty ordered. Then, an even more intense pain shot up my leg. "There we go. I got the little cocksucker."

Richie quickly turned his head to look away from my leg, and then panic seized me. Dusty turned to look at me and said something that sounded like, "It should be all better now." But I barely heard him, because when he turned, I was staring at my leg.

The right leg of my jeans was rolled up, showing a large section of road rash that spanned from my shoe up over my knee. It looked like the times when I used to scrape my palms after falling off of my skateboard, only much, much worse. Most of the scrape was red with fresh blood, but parts of it looked black. I could see flecks of sand scattered throughout. When I saw my wound, the walls of the train seemed to start closing in on me, and I felt dizzy.

"Had to get the big pieces out," Dusty grinned. In two bloody fingers, he held up a piece of rock that was about one inch in diameter. Lodged between his thumb and the rock, I saw a small flap of my skin dangling. A second later, my head fell back, and I passed out once again.

* * *

When I finally came to again, my leg had calmed to a dull throb, and there was hardly any pain in my shoulder now. Richie and Dusty were sitting in the opposite corner of the gondola, talking low. I spared a glance down and noticed that the pant leg was still rolled up, but something black was wrapped around my wound. When I looked closer, I recognized it as my Whitesnake T-shirt.

"What if it gets infected?" I heard Richie ask Dusty.

"We'll just have to cross that bridge when we come to it," Dusty answered. He looked over at me and saw that I was awake and propped up on my elbows. "Hey, boy, don't get up too fast."

"You okay, Shelly?" Richie asked, walking over to me. He looked funny, balancing on the slanted sides of the vibrating train car with his arms held out.

I tried to speak, but nothing came out. I was parched. Richie repeated his question, and I nodded in answer. He squatted next to me and held out a bottle of water to me. I accepted it thankfully and swallowed a gulp of water.

"Don't drink too much. That's gotta last us," Dusty said, followed by a hail of those vicious coughs. This batch must have produced some nasty sputum, because he wrinkled his nose and spat disgustedly.

"How long was I passed out for?" I asked, feeling a little refreshed from the water.

"Not too long, man. I thought you were a goner. It's a good thing I took a shit back in Pennsylvania, because if I didn't, I'd be cleaning my underwear right now," Richie said.

I laughed dryly and gazed up at the sky above us. The clouds and the treetops rolled by soundlessly. I could still hear the loud clickety-clacks of the train's wheels reverberating off the steel walls of the car, but my ears seemed to have adjusted to it a little.

Shivering, I sat up and scooted over so that I could lean on the side of the train car. As soon as I moved, the skin on my leg felt as if someone had scoured it with a cheese grater.

"I'm hungry," I said, trying to ignore the pain. My stomach was indeed growling.

"Sorry, son, you'll have to wait a little longer," Dusty empathized. "I only have enough food for myself for about four small meals. I'll have to ration it out between the three of us, so we'll have to skip a couple meals to last us the whole trip."

"*Four meals?* How the hell long are we going to be on this train?" I asked.

"Oh, it'll be about fifteen hours or so," he answered flatly.

"How do you even know that?"

"I ride this line all the time, son," he said with an unmistakable tinge of pride.

"Where the hell are we going anyway for it to take that long?"

"Dusty said he's been staying at a camp," Richie answered. "Well, *he* called it a hobo jungle. It's in Mississippi."

I searched through my mind, trying to remember where the hell Mississippi was. In my head, I pictured the road atlas and recalled that it was about two states northeast of Mexico. *At least we're headed in the right direction,* I thought.

"Yep, I told yer brother here that y'all can stay as long as you want," Dusty offered. "We've built ourselves quite a little community there. We've got a lake, shelter, and even a mountain spring for water. Most of us bring food whenever we can. I would have brought some back with me this time, but I was in Virginia for … other reasons. Anyway, it may not be Buckingham Palace, but it's a place to stay until y'all figger out what you're gonna do."

Richie nodded at me, showing his approval. I was surprised, considering his earlier behavior, but I guessed he was starting to trust Dusty a little. I nodded back, figuring it was our only choice anyway. Dusty got up and balanced comically over to the opposite corner again, coughing and hacking the whole way. Richie and I watched him as he rooted through his tattered rucksack until he found what he was looking for. He pulled out a thick paperback book called *The Fountainhead* by Ayn Rand. The spine was riddled with wrinkles, and the pages were dog-eared. He was soon engrossed in his novel, and that was when I whispered to Richie.

"So you trust this guy, right?"

"I don't know, Shelly. I guess we don't have much of a choice right now, though. But I guess he seems all right," Richie whispered back. "I think that this is probably the best way. It's a lot closer to Mexico for one thing."

"I agree. We can go to this camp and stay there for a while to plan out what we're gonna do next."

"Well, I'm a little nervous about staying in a strange place with a bunch of strange people, man. But I'm hoping that once we get there, maybe Dusty can teach us how to hotwire a car, if he knows how. Then we can be back on the road again."

"I don't know if I agree with stealing some poor schmuck's car, but I guess if there's no other choice, we'll have to. He might also know a good spot to find another train, though. One that goes into Mexico."

"Good thinking, man."

"I'll tell you one thing though. I can't believe we hopped a train," I marveled.

"Yeah, I know. It was pretty heavy."

"How heavy?" I asked with a grin.

"Super, ultra, mega heavy," he replied, smiling back at me.

We had come up with the phrase "super, ultra, mega heavy" a couple of months ago. It was used to describe things that were just too intense for one adjective, such as Slayer's newest album, *Seasons in the Abyss*, or the Patrick Swayze blockbuster we saw that summer called *Point Break*. I was happy to get a reaction from Richie, though. It was good to see him smile.

As the day drew on, the wind blowing around us began to get colder and colder. Richie and I put some extra layers on and donned our jackets as well. As I leaned against the cold, hard steel of the train car, I took Tiffany's note from my pocket and read it again. *I never got to tell her my answer*, I thought. I smelled the note to see if

I could catch a whiff of her sweet perfume, but it only smelled like paper.

Later, Dusty rationed two turkey sandwiches on hoagie rolls three ways, and we all ate together. We asked him some more questions about being a hobo and about the hobo jungle. He answered every one of them with patience and then asked a few of his own. We told him how we had run away from home, leaving out every detail relating to Jim. We also explained how we had all of our money stolen from us in Connecticut. He told us that he understood, because he, too, had run away when he was younger and had never looked back. We kept up the façade of being brothers to make things simple. Besides, we liked it.

When night fell, the air in the gondola felt frigid, so Richie and I huddled together to keep warm. The three of us talked a little longer. Dusty told us some of his "road stories" between fits of coughing, and Richie and I listened in awe.

Sometime later, my eyelids felt heavy, and despite the throbbing in my leg and the annoying clamor of the train, I slept.

*   *   *

The morning was cold and damp, and my skin felt hot around the eyes. The throbs in my leg pounded furiously, giving me a headache. The sound of Dusty's coughing attack was what woke me up. It was so violent that I thought that he was either choking or dying—maybe both. I looked over at him when he stopped coughing. He was sitting at the opposite corner of the gondola, reading his book. Beside me, I was surprised to see that Richie was still sleeping peacefully, a slight twinge of smile on his lips. Whatever he was dreaming about, it must have been pleasant.

I yawned and stretched and then stood up. Pleased that I was able to put weight on my leg without it hurting too badly, I hobbled carefully over to Dusty. As I sat down beside him, he held his index finger up, telling me to hold on. He read for a minute longer, finding a good place to stop. Then he inserted his shoddy bookmark and put the book on top of his rucksack.

"That's a thick book," I said. "Is it any good?"

"It's a classic," Dusty stated. "This is my third time reading it."

"What's it about?"

"Architects."

"That sounds boring."

"Not at all," he said.

"So you're into architecture?"

"No."

"Then, why would you read a book about architects?" I asked.

"Well, it's not just about architects. It's more about takin' a stand against the establishment, not compromisin' yer personal vision, and thinkin' for yerself, if you will. Thinkin' outside of the box, as people say nowadays."

I was more than impressed with Dusty. My first impression of him was that he was an uneducated, lazy Southerner. Apparently, that was just my Northerner stereotype. There certainly seemed to be more to Dusty than met the eye; however, I didn't think what people thought of him mattered to him either way. In fact, I had the feeling that he liked people to perceive him the way I originally had.

"Why didn't you just say that in the first place?" I asked.

"Well, it was the short answer, 'cause I didn't think y'all came over here to talk about *The Fountainhead*."

"Fair enough. I wanted to ask you why you're helping us. You're even sharing your food with us. It just seems weird to me."

Dusty eased his head back and laughed cheerfully. "Are y'all that disconnected from humanity, boy? Y'all don't think there are good people on this earth still? I can't say I blame you much, I guess. The world seems to be goin' to hell in a hand basket. But I can tell you that there are still some of us out there that believe in helpin' out a fellow man. Besides, I don't like to see young people suffering."

I let his words sink in for a moment. I tried searching his eyes to see if he was just bullshitting me, but they held my gaze confidently. Here was this older man, one who looked like society had chewed him up and squeezed him out of its anus, yet he still cared about people. My brain told me that it just didn't add up, but my heart told me that he was for real. He was right. I was jaded. I didn't believe there were any Good Samaritans left in the world.

"Can I ask you something else, Dusty?"

"Sure thing," he said. "This will be what y'all *really* came over here to talk to me about, right?"

I felt my cheeks getting hot. "Um, yeah I guess. It's just that I noticed that you're coughing up blood a lot. Isn't that bad? Are you going to be okay?"

He bowed his head for a moment and then looked back up at me with hard resolve.

"Don't really know, boy. And I don't really care. I've lived my life as good as I can, and I can only hope that I will die just as good."

"What do you mean by that?" I asked.

"I'm just sayin' that we never know when our time's comin'. You could have been pulled under the train wheels yesterday, and your time would have been up. Just like that." He snapped his fingers to emphasize his point. "I just hope that when it's *my* time, I can die gracefully and as painlessly as possible, preferably on a train." He then let out a hoarse laugh that ended in another violent spasm of coughs and another chunk of bloody spit in the corner.

The noise woke Richie up, and he made his way over to us. His hair was a tangled bird's nest from using his backpack as a pillow. It made me wonder what my own hair looked like.

"Dusty, how will we know when to jump off?" Richie asked.

"Well, the reason this train is empty is 'cause it's on its way back to Mississippi to pick up another load. That's also why it's movin' a little faster than it does with a full load. Our camp is about a click short of the Mississippi station. We'll be jumpin' out after we feel the train startin' to slow down on its approach to said station."

"Do you think Shelly will be okay jumping out with his bad leg?"

"I dunno, but he's gonna *have* to be okay. If he's still in the train when it gets to the station, he'll be hauled off by the bulls just as soon as they find him. My best advice is to make sure y'all land on both feet, but when you fall—and you *will* fall, trust me—try to roll onto yer good side first. Speakin' of yer leg, we'd better change the dressin' on it."

It wasn't as painful as I thought it would be. Dusty removed the "dressing" from my shin and replaced it with another one of my T-shirts. Thankfully, I was able to look at the abrasion this time without passing out. The bleeding had stopped, and it had already started to scab over. In a few of the scab's creases, a clear yellowish puss leaked out. Dusty told me that the wound looked slightly infected. He said it was at risk of a more serious infection, if I didn't keep it clean. Obviously, that was not possible in our current situation, but he indicated that there was a stash of medical supplies at the hobo jungle, which might include Neosporin.

* * *

A couple of hours later, Dusty rationed out the rest of his food, which turned out to be another pair of turkey sandwiches. We sat around in a circle and ate peacefully as we talked of inconsequential things. After we finished our food, Dusty returned to his corner and began reading his book again. Richie and I lay down on our backs and watched the clouds roll by. He told me that he felt a little better about Dusty. He explained that if Dusty was going to try to hurt us or something, he probably would have tried it by now. He also said that he was grateful to Dusty for taking care of my leg.

I had lost all track of time and all sense of where I was while on that train. The only thing I knew for sure was that my leg burned and throbbed, and I was growing absolutely sick and tired of the wind blowing in my face. What made the wind worse was the occasional bug that would fly into my face. At the high speed, it felt like a nasty bee sting each time.

Sometime after we ate, the train finally started to slow down.

Dusty told me to roll my pant leg over my "dressing" so it wouldn't get dirty when I fell after the jump. I looked at Richie beside me, and the crazy bastard was grinning like a kid waiting for the ice cream truck. A nervous laugh escaped me, and I wondered what the hell I was doing. I was about to jump off of a moving train.

Icy fingers played Chopin on my spine as I gathered up my backpack and duffel bag.

"Time to shit or get off the pot, Shelly," Richie yelled over the screeching metal. Part of me felt that it might just be better to get off the pot.

Chapter 11
TRAIN TOWN

September 1991

"Remember to tuck your head and roll, boys!" Dusty shouted. He hoisted himself onto the lip of the gondola and threw his rucksack over the side. The wind blew his hat off and revealed a balding head with strands of gray hair swirling around. "Cocksucker!" he yelled and then leaped off the side of train car.

We clambered up to watch him. He landed on his feet and fell onto his side, rolling back toward his ejected rucksack. After he came to a stop, he stood up quickly and brushed himself off. He looked back at us in anticipation. Richie instructed me to go first this time, and my feet suddenly felt like they were glued to the train.

"I can't, Richie," I pleaded. "Let's just stay in here. Maybe they won't find us in here, and we can jump out when it stops."

"Shelly, you know they'll find us. Dusty said there are hands all over the train as soon as it stops at the station, and they search every car," Richie argued impatiently. "You have to jump, man. It'll be okay. I can't get caught, man. I *won't* get caught. Please ... just fucking jump ... *now!*"

I closed my eyes and found myself thinking of the time when my father had taught me how to swim. When I was five years old, my parents rented a house on Lake Winnipesaukee. At the water's edge, a wooden dock extended out onto the water. My father and John were already in the water, and I was standing on the edge of the dock, shivering. I remember gazing into the cloudy water rippling around my father's chest as he yelled for me to jump. "Come on, Shelton. Your brother did it with no problem. Why can't you just trust me? I'll catch you," my father coaxed. When I jumped, he caught me with his strong arms, and everything turned out okay just like he had said.

As I kept that moment in mind, I threw my bags over the side of the train and jumped before doubt could settle in again. For a split second, I felt as if I was suspended in midair, and the racket of the train was completely gone, replaced only by the sound of the wind. Then, the ground rushed toward me faster than I thought it would have, and my feet hit, sending a painful ripping sensation through my injured leg on impact. Remembering what Dusty had told me, I bent my knees and lunged forward into a roll. The wind was knocked from me as I rolled, and I felt a rock dig into my back; however, I came to a stop seconds later, virtually unharmed.

When I stood up and looked back, Richie was already rolling on the ground. I waited for him while he got up and retrieved his bags. When he reached me, he threw his head back, laughing and howling wildly. I felt giddy, too, and chuckled in relief. What an adrenaline rush!

We walked back toward Dusty, who was coughing as usual and searching for his hat, and I collected my bags along the way. The last couple of train cars screeched past us as we made it to Dusty. I scanned the area and saw that both sides of the train tracks were flanked with a green sea of wooded terrain. The contrast in temperature was astounding to me. On the train, especially during the night, the constant wind rushing by made the air frigid and annoying. Off of the train, however, the Mississippi air was hot and thick without even a semblance of a breeze.

Dusty finally found his hat and brushed it off before he placed it back on his head. He told us to follow him as he headed into the woods. We passed two trees with symbols carved in their trunks. The first one looked like the male gender symbol turned on its side, so the arrow pointed horizontally to the right instead of diagonally upward. The second one was comprised of a squiggly line that looked like waves, and beneath that were a circle, an X, and another circle.

"What do those symbols mean, Dusty?" I asked as we trudged through the thick woods.

"The first one tells hoboes to go 'this way,' and the second one promises fresh water and a safe campsite up ahead," he revealed.

"So what exactly is this hobo jungle anyway? Do you guys have a big screen TV and a swimming pool?" Richie asked.

Sighing, Dusty answered, "This ain't a four-star hotel, young man. It's a clearin' in the woods beside an old train graveyard. And no, we don't have a pool, but we got a lake. This place is a sanctuary for the destitute, and y'all should show it some respect, bein' of destitution yerself."

"What's a train graveyard?" I asked, trying to alleviate some of Richie's sarcasm.

"It's where trains go when they die," Dusty grinned.

"I think I've heard of that," Richie said. "It's like a junkyard for trains, right?"

"Exactly. You'll see it up ahead. We've built ourselves a place where hoboes from all over can come and stay for as long as they want to. There are a couple of rules that we go by to keep it a civilized society. And like I said before, there's a lake to wash in. There's also a mountain with a spring that gives us our water, and everyone pitches in to bring in food to the camp one way or another."

"What rules do you have?" I asked.

"Well, first of all, everyone has to pitch in. No one stays for free. We share the workload. Everyone either volunteers or is assigned to do things like gather firewood, collect water from the spring, or find and share food. Secondly, no hobo is allowed to steal from another hobo in the camp. We frown upon thievery in general, except when necessary."

Ahead of me, Richie swatted at a bug flying around his head as he traversed the woods behind Dusty. I lifted the bottom of my shirt and fanned it up and down in a futile attempt to cool myself off from the sweltering Mississippi air. I noticed that aside from the occasional bird chirping, everything seemed so silent, probably because my ears had gotten so accustomed to the train noise. When I started to feel hot pain starting up in my leg again, I looked down and saw that fresh blood had seeped through my jeans. The impact from the train jump must have split open some of the scabs.

After a small bout of coughing, Dusty continued his explanation. "Most of us work, too. We go into town and do odd jobs for people, makin' a couple dollars here and there. That money is always put back into our little society here for food, medical supplies, and blankets. And one of my personal pet peeves is that any pots or pans must be cleaned after usin' them."

"You don't save up the money to like … buy a car or something?" Richie inquired.

"No, a true hobo puts personal freedom before any desire for worldly gain, son. Bein' a hobo is a way of life. We get a couple of bad eggs comin' through here every once in a while, though. Some of 'em are disrespectful types who break the rules. Some of 'em are wannabe hoboes, just spendin' time around us. Slummin' it, if you will. But then they go back to their cushy homes and jobs. We call them 'yuppie hoboes' or 'recreational riders.'"

I couldn't help but wonder if Dusty had ever worked a steady job and lived in a house. I was pretty sure that he probably had, but I didn't want to ask him. To acknowledge that and talk about it seemed as if it would tarnish my view of Dusty and violate his privacy. I was beginning to think of him as an old wise man who was leading us to a promised land.

We followed him out of the woods and into a clearing, and he turned around to look at us. As he spread his arms open in a welcoming gesture, he jovially told us, "Welcome to Train Town, boys."

I was astonished at what I saw.

Row upon row of decommissioned trains lined the entire left-hand side of the clearing. The skeletal remains of these hulking behemoths sat silently in rust, forgotten by the world. There were several different types of cabooses, engines, grainers, and boxcars.

Some were slightly damaged, and some were smashed; but all were rusty. They spent their eternal rest on rusted tracks that joined up beyond the rows and extended into the overgrowth behind. Past the overgrowth, the tracks disappeared into the surrounding woods, where the train station presumably presided. Weeds and high grass sprouted up between the train cars, and some of the plants even grew through the rusted holes in their floors.

The right-hand side of the clearing donned a cluster of tents loosely surrounding a large fire pit with various pots and cooking utensils suspended over it. Most of the tents looked sturdy, but on closer inspection, I saw that they were actually ragged and frayed. Several hoboes could be seen either milling around the camp area and tending to various tasks or sitting outside of their tents and talking. Beyond the tents, the overgrowth gave way to a thick, wooded area that gradually rose up into a mountain.

In the center, separating the rows of dead trains from the tents, sat a patch of trampled grass leading to a single train car. The car was situated at an angle along the tree line opposite of where we were standing. It was shiny silver, with considerably less rust than the other cars. The words "Flying Yankee" were emblazoned on the front of it. Beside this isolated locomotive was a path that led into the woods.

"That's the Yankee Flyer," Dusty said after he followed my gaze toward the isolated train car. "And beside that is the pathway to Lake Iroquois, where we fish, bathe, and wash clothes."

"Yankee Flyer? I think I've heard that name before," I said.

"The name's been used fer all kinds of different things, but it was originally a train that was built in the thirties fer use in New England," Dusty explained.

"New England?" Richie and I looked at each other. "What is it doing down here in Mississippi?"

"No one around here really knows. Interesting, ain't it? Yep, the ole Yankee Flyer was decommissioned in the fifties. We like to keep this one up nicely. That's why it's not as rundown as the other cars. It's kinda like our own monument, sort of a Statue of Liberty for Train Town, if you will," Dusty said proudly.

I spotted a symbol chalked on a small board propped up on a rock. The symbol resembled an upside-down football goal post.

"What does that mean?" I asked.

"Simply put, it means 'here is the place,'" Dusty replied. "Follow me, and I'll introduce you to some of the 'boes."

Dusty walked three steps and then exploded into another of his violent coughing fits. As he coughed, he swayed on his feet and then dropped to his knees. Richie and I ran over to him to see if he was all right. When I put my hand on his shoulder, he shrugged it off and yelled at us to get away. He continued coughing up several batches of blood-filled sputum until he finally calmed down and got to his feet.

"Dusty, are you all right?" Richie asked.

"Yeah, yeah, I'm fine. Must be the goddamned cigarettes gettin' to me again," Dusty grumbled. Ironically, he stuffed a cigarette in his mouth and fumbled around for his lighter.

He resumed walking again toward the tents and made it this time. As we approached, a pear-shaped man of about seventy years hobbled over to us. He had scraggly white hair that sat carelessly over his ears, white stubble on his face, and drooping jowls. He wore dirty khaki pants and an orange hunting vest. His hands were adorned with fingerless gloves.

"Ho, there, Dusty Rails," said the man.

"Boys, this here is Eleventeen Eddie. Most of us just call him E.E. for short, though. He's the de facto mayor of Train Town," Dusty said. He pointed to me and then Richie. "This here's Shelton, and this here's Richie."

"Nice to meet you boys," E.E. greeted, shaking our hands. I detected a slight New York accent similar to Richie's. He looked at Dusty sideways and said, "Dusty, I've never known you to be a Jocker."

Richie tensed up beside me and glared at the two men. On the train, Dusty had explained some of the more salty hobo terms like Jocker, which basically translated to pervert. I didn't understand what Richie's problem was—obviously, Dusty wasn't a pervert—but I made a mental note to ask him about it later.

"It's not like that," Dusty snapped. "These are good boys who were in a not-so-good life and decided to take life by the horns and go their own way."

"Commendable," E.E. granted. "Well, let's introduce you to some of the other 'boes. If you'll be staying here, then it's best you meet the staples of Train Town."

E.E. ushered us around the area, introducing us to a few hoboes who all had very colorful names. There was Beef Wellington, who was a large and hairy man; Fat Neck Charlie, whose neck skin hung loosely like a rooster's wattle; Chuck Norris, who looked nothing like the real Chuck Norris and had only one visible tooth in his mouth; and Beans Mahoney, who had only one arm and wore dark-rimmed glasses and a bowler's hat.

Each of the men we met was very kind and forthcoming. Richie, on the other hand, was distant and standoffish. He seemed suspicious of every person.

At some point, during our tour of Train Town, Dusty had wandered off. When I turned around and asked where he had gone, E.E. told me that Dusty went to his tent to rest. Although I had only known Dusty for two days, I already considered him a friend and felt worried for him. I wasn't a doctor, but I knew that coughing up blood was something serious.

When I felt my leg singing to me in its painful voice again, I remembered that Dusty had told us there were likely medical supplies in the camp. I asked E.E. about it, and he told me that a hobo named Navy Neal was in charge of the camp's medical supplies. E.E. then asked around for him and was told that he was down at the lake. He led us down a long path through the woods behind the Yankee Flyer. Along the way, we met up with Navy Neal.

"Ho, Navy Neal," E.E. called out to him.

He was a big man who stood about six feet and three inches, with salt-and-pepper-colored hair that was wet from the lake. His eyes were a brown so dark that they looked almost black, and he had a broad chin and a beaklike nose. He was wearing a damp blue T-shirt that bore an eagle in front of a U.S. flag, clutching an anchor in its talons. What stuck out most was the large tattoo on his left forearm. It was an aerial view of large red turtle with three white dolphins swimming side-by-side on its back.

"Hey Eleventeen Eddie, whattaya say?" Navy Neal replied. His eyes met mine, and he smiled at me.

"This is Shelton and Richie, brought here by Dusty Rails," E.E. informed. I shook Navy Neal's hand and moved aside so Richie could do so as well. When he did, he glowered at the man and eyed him suspiciously. "Shelton here tells me that he has quite a scrape along his leg that's in danger of becoming infected. Do you have any Neosporin left?"

"Oh, sure I do. But you'll want to clean your wound with a little soap and water first. Why don't you boys go get washed up down at the lake? You look like hell," Navy Neal said, chuckling merrily. He hadn't seemed to have noticed Richie's glare, or perhaps he simply chose to ignore it. "E.E. can show you the rest of the way down to the lake. Here, you can take my soap. There you go. And when you boys are done washing up, Richie here can go see E.E. to set up a tent for you guys. I think we have a spare somewhere. Shelton, you can come to my tent, and I'll fix you up. Does that sound good to go across the board?"

I nodded in agreement, but Richie hastily interjected. "Maybe Shelly can wait until after we set up the tent, so I can go with him."

"Don't be silly, Richie," I said. I was a little annoyed that he thought I needed my hand held. I couldn't understand why Richie was being so apprehensive about everything. "I'll be fine."

Navy Neal then set out back to the camp, and E.E. walked us farther down the trail until we came to the lake. The shore was a small patch of sand surrounded by overgrowth and trees on all sides. The lake itself looked pretty small to me, more like a huge pond. As I looked into the water, I was impressed at how clear it was. I could see the bottom from where I was standing. E.E. told us that we would have to use our clean clothes as towels, because there were no spares in the camp. Towels were a much sought after commodity in Train Town, limited to those who were able to secure one from a laundry line in the town.

E.E. left us to ourselves, and that was when I laid into Richie.

"Dude, what's going on with you?" I asked. "Why are you being so rude? These people seem fine."

"How do you know that, Shelly? You don't know what's going on in people's heads."

"What do you mean? Why can't we give them the benefit of the doubt?" I asked, borrowing a phrase from my mother.

"Oh, yeah? What about those two assholes at Burger King? They got the benefit of the doubt," Richie said, raising his voice.

I sighed. He was right to a certain extent. We had to be careful, but at the same time, I wasn't up for more travelling. Besides, I trusted Dusty, and I had faith that he wouldn't have brought us here if it was dangerous.

"Yeah, I know. But my leg hurts man. And I'm exhausted. Plus, everyone here seems really nice," I said. "You trust Dusty, don't you?"

"Yes," he said and then added, "but I didn't trust him right away."

"But my point is that Dusty wouldn't bring us to a bad place, man. He trusts these people, so why shouldn't we?"

"Because Dusty doesn't know what's going on in people's heads either! Like that guy Navy Neal. Don't you think he seemed a little ... off?"

I thought about it for a second and then shook my head. "Navy Neal seems like an all right guy to me."

"I'm telling you I got a really bad vibe from him," Richie continued. "I don't think we should just trust people right off the bat. It's not smart. In fact, it's stupid! It's really stupid!"

"Not everyone is a bad person, Richie," I snapped. "Not everyone is Jim!"

As soon as I said it, I wished that I hadn't. Richie narrowed his eyes at me, angry and hurt, and he folded his arms in front of him defensively. After a moment of thinking about what to say next, I chose my words carefully. I needed to defuse the situation. We needed to stick together, not fight.

"Look, I didn't mean to go there, okay? I'm sorry," I said softly.

"It's just that I don't see anything wrong with getting a little help." He just shrugged, so I continued, "I think this place is okay. It's not like we're going to get robbed again. We don't have any more money. So what else could happen?"

Richie looked up at the sky, apparently deep in thought. I surveyed the calm lake water, waiting for him to talk. I tried to imagine what he was thinking about, but I couldn't. I understood that he was probably still shook up about killing Jim—I know I was—but what did that have to do with Train Town? I was trying my best to see Richie as my best friend and not a killer, and here he was, thinking everyone else was some sort of psycho. I wondered if maybe that was how it felt after you kill someone. Maybe you started thinking that if you could do it, anyone could.

He turned toward me and looked like he was about to say something. Some of the color had faded from his face, and he seemed on the verge of tears again. Then, he abruptly closed his mouth and cleared his throat. His face seemed to harden in that moment. He looked as though he had aged twenty years right in front of my face. Somehow, it seemed like an epic battle of emotions was being waged behind his eyes.

"I don't know, dude," he said flatly. "I don't know anything anymore."

"Are you okay? What's wrong?"

"Nothing," he said with a dismissive wave of his hand. "I guess I'll just leave it up to you, Shelly. Your head is probably clearer than mine right now."

"Are you sure?"

"Yeah, I'm sorry. I just got a lot on my mind. And you're right, man. Not everyone is Jim. I'll try to keep that in mind."

"Thanks, Richie. I'll tell you what. If we notice anyone going crazy, swinging axes around or something, we'll just leave, okay? Plus, you have the gun. I'm sure if you wave that around, whoever is bothering us will stop in a hurry."

Richie chuckled. "Okay, deal. Hey, no one can see us with all these woods around, right?"

"No, I don't think so," I said, looking around.

"Okay, then. Last one in is a rotten egg," he said.

He quickly began to strip off his clothes, and I followed his example, anticipating the cold rush of the water. We raced into the lake, smiling and yelling the whole way. Richie dove in first, and I followed, laughing so hard that I swallowed some water. When I came up out of the water, Richie jumped on me and dunked me under again. This time, I kept my mouth closed, because thinking about how many dirty hoboes had bathed in that water made me feel nauseous.

Richie and I swam for a while, losing track of the hours, having the time of our lives. My leg was stinging during our swim, but I didn't care. It was good to see Richie smiling again. Hell, it was good to feel myself smiling. The water wasn't as cold as I had expected, though. I was used to the frigid New Hampshire lakes and oceans, where even in the summer, you felt like you were going to have a heart attack when you jumped in. Nevertheless, it was refreshing.

Finally, we got tired of horsing around and washed ourselves. I soon found out that bathing in a lake was much different than taking a shower. Even after I had lathered my skin up with the soap and dunked myself under the water, the soapy film still remained. I had to squat down and rub my skin under the water to remove the soap. I also made sure to be extra careful washing my leg, because rubbing it too hard was painful and I didn't want it to start bleeding again.

When we were finished washing ourselves, we washed each other's backs and joked about it, calling each other names to maintain our masculinity. When we got out, we dried ourselves off with our clean clothes and then put them on. It felt good to be clean and to be wearing clean clothes. After all, I hadn't showered or changed in two days.

We made our way back up the path and into the camp. Finding E.E.'s tent was easy, as he was standing in front of it. He told us that Richie and I would have to share a tent, because they only had one spare in the entire camp. That was fine by us, we told him. I asked him which tent belonged to Navy Neal, and he pointed at a large tent farther out toward the mountain. *Should have known it would be navy blue,* I thought with a chuckle.

Navy Neal was lying on a blanket in his tent, reading a book called *Treason's Harbour* by Patrick O'Brian. He put his book down and stood up when I ducked into the tent. He had to hunch over, because he was too tall for the tent. He reached behind me and zipped down the tent.

"Okay, Shelton. So what happened to your leg?" He asked.

"I was hopping … uh, catching out, I mean … and I didn't bring my leg up in time. I was dragged along for a little ways, and it scraped me up pretty good," I said. "Dusty told me that it's in danger of being infected. There's some puss coming out a little. Sorry, I don't mean to be gross."

"Don't worry, boy. After some of the things I've seen and heard in the Navy, nothing grosses me out anymore," he assured with a grin. "So come on and take off your pants so I can get a look-see."

"Well, I think it's just at the bottom here," I said, rolling up my pant leg.

"When you were dragged, you may have scraped it up farther, too. I need to take a look and put Neosporin on the whole scrape, not just part of it," Navy Neal explained. "Besides, I did time as a medical officer in the Navy, boy. You don't have anything I haven't seen before. Don't be a sissy."

I hesitated for a moment and then decided he was right. *There's no reason for me to be all girly and shy about it*, I thought. I unzipped and unbuttoned my jeans and then pulled them off. I carefully removed the Van Halen T-shirt that was wrapped around my leg and then stood there, shivering in my T-shirt and underwear. Navy Neal squatted down in front of me and examined my abrasion. It looked a little better than it had before—now that it was clean at least—but it still was pretty nasty. I noted only a small scratch above the knee. Other than that, the brunt of the wound spread from below my knee and down to my ankle.

"Is it infected?" I asked.

"A little bit, yes. You were battered a smidge, but overall, I don't think too much damage was done. There's only one area of concern right here above the ankle. It looks a little deep."

"Yeah, I think that's where Dusty pulled out a little rock," I indicated and then added, "I passed out when I saw it."

Navy Neal laughed heartily and slapped his knee. "Well, if you feel like passing out in here, don't take the tent down with you."

"I'll try not to."

"All right, now hang on a second, and I'll get the Neosporin. I'll also get some gauze and bandage to wrap around it. Van Halen may be a great band, but their T-shirts are definitely not proper dressing. We need to keep this clean and covered."

Navy Neal dug around in a cardboard banker's box in the corner of his tent. He seemed like a nice enough guy to me, but something in his eyes freaked me out a little. I couldn't pinpoint exactly what it was. I shook it off though, realizing that it was probably just Richie's initial suspicions wearing off on me.

He brought out a half-used tube of Neosporin and began smearing it gently into my road rash. He took great care not to cause a lot of pain, and I was happy for that. When he was finished, he placed a patch of gauze on the scrape and began wrapping my leg in a bandage, starting at the ankle. He wrapped farther up as well, leaving my knee uncovered so it would be able to bend, and stopped in the middle of my thigh. I wasn't sure that he needed to cover the little scratch on my thigh, but I remained silent. He seemed to know what he was doing, so who was I to argue?

He told me to hold the edge of the bandage, and then he applied tape to hold it down. As he was taping, the edge of his arm grazed against my crotch and lingered long enough to make me feel uncomfortable. I jerked back a little at his touch, and he looked up at me with a wide grin and said, "Sorry, kid, I didn't mean anything by it." He finished taping me up and put his medical supplies away. I scrambled around, pulling my jeans back on. I felt quite disturbed and slightly confused.

There seemed to be no logical reason why his arm should have rubbed across me down there. It gave me a shameful, sort of queasy feeling that left me unsettled. He had apologized and said that he hadn't meant anything by it, but it had still happened. It didn't even seem to have affected him, so I assumed that I was just overthinking the whole ordeal. It was just the look on his face when he said sorry to me. His wide grin and dark eyes seemed almost to say, "What are you gonna do about it, kid?"

"Is there something wrong, Shelton? Did I make the bandage too tight?" Navy Neal asked, showing concern.

"Uh … no, it's fine. I was just … somewhere else," I stammered. I shook my head and decided I wasn't going to let it bother me. It was over. It was an accident. "I'm sorry. I'm just very tired from traveling."

"Well, your brother and E.E. should be done putting up your tent by now, so maybe you can get some rest. And keep that leg clean, understand?"

I told him yes and then left the tent. I could still feel Navy Neal's touch on my crotch as I made my way over to Richie, or maybe that was all in my head. Seeing Richie helped combat the awkward feeling, though. I didn't say anything to him about the incident with Navy Neal. It was too embarrassing. Besides, the more I thought about it, the more my concern over the matter seemed silly.

Richie was bringing our bags into the newly erected tent, a faded red one of modest size. I could see no visible defects, which appeased my concerns about rain and bugs. Richie looked as exhausted as I was, so I suggested that we get a couple of hours of sleep. Inside our tent, we used our bags as pillows just as we had done on the train.

Neither of us, however, was able to sleep. It was still daylight, which made it harder to keep our eyes closed. Plus, it was a strange situation. We were used to sleeping in our beds, in our houses, in our quiet little town. It was a little exciting, too, being in this bizarre place. There were new and unusual people all around us. *Hoboes!*

We could hear their laughter and mumbled discussions through the tent, but mostly, we heard Dusty's violent coughing. His attacks seemed to be getting closer and closer together, and I found myself feeling genuinely worried for him. With each terrible hacking cough, Richie and I looked at each other in concern, knowing that if Dusty didn't get medical attention soon, he would most likely die.

* * *

A couple of hours later, E.E. came to our tent to invite us to dinner. We joined him and a slew of other hoboes at the fire pit. They were sitting in a loose circle around the fire, where a large pot was suspended over the flame. When I saw Navy Neal, I tensed at first, but then I told myself to stop being stupid. E.E. told us that the pot contained "Mulligan Stew," which was a little bit of everything. Each hobo contributed whatever they could to the stew: a carrot that they had pulled from a garden in town, a scrap of bacon or some hamburger that had been scoffed from the market, or a few stalks of celery given by the priest at the church in town. It actually turned out to be quite tasty.

As we ate, most of the other hoboes made us feel welcome. I was pleased to see that Richie was making an effort at being friendly. The dinner was filled with talks about some of the more comical adventures that they had been through.

Beef Wellington told everyone how he had ripped a hole in the crotch of his favorite pants as he was hopping a fence to evade the bulls at a train station in Tennessee. He said that the bulls were doubled over with laughter when he tumbled onto the ground with his willy waggling out.

Chuck Norris complained about being shot in the ass with birdshot over in Kentucky when he was jumping out of the window of some rich woman's house. He said her husband had come home and that he had not been too happy seeing his wife bumping uglies with a dirty hobo.

Fat Neck Charlie spoke of his days riding the rails up in Canada, saying, "The Canuck women up there are more apt to give a hobo herpes than a slice of bread." Each story was received with resounding laughter around the fire. Richie and I weren't sure what some of the bawdier things meant, but we laughed along with everyone else anyway.

Dusty joined us at some point during the dinner. His face was pale and sickly, but he seemed cheery enough. He laughed at the funny things that were said, some of his laughs even dissolving without a cough, and he contributed some of his own outrageous road tales.

As it got darker, most of the hoboes went back to their tents. A handful of them stayed around the fire with us. There was Dusty, E.E., Navy Neal, and two guys we hadn't been introduced to yet. One of them was a black man they called Mr. Smurf. He had a beard and short hair, and he wore a dark green army jacket and fatigues. The other one, Chancellor Bismarck, spoke in a German accent and had matted-down blond hair with a mustache. He had an aviator jacket slung over his shoulders.

"Vere are you boyz from?" Chancellor Bismarck asked, lighting a big fat cigar.

Richie and I hadn't spoken or been spoken to very much during the dinner, so at first, we didn't realize he was talking to us.

"Oh, us? Uh … we're from New York. Yeah, New York," Richie said.

"That's where I'm originally from," E.E. said.

"Yeah, E.E. here's a regular old American nomad," Mr. Smurf piped in.

"Yep, I've been around," E.E. replied.

"How come you're called Mr. Smurf?" I asked.

"Simply put, because I like *The Smurfs*."

"By the way, Mr. Smurf, there's something I've been meaning to ask you," Navy Neal said, looking at us and grinning. "In the whole village, why was there only one female Smurf?"

"Why you always gotta be dissin' *The Smurfs*, man?" Mr. Smurf asked, half-amused and half-irritated.

"It's a legitimate question. I've always wondered if Smurfette was the village whore or if maybe all of the other Smurfs were just gay and she was their fag hag," Navy Neal teased.

"Actually, there were eventually *three* female Smurfs," I corrected. "There was Smurfette, Sassette, and Nanny Smurf."

Navy Neal shot me a quick, annoyed glance.

"Well, there you go," Mr. Smurf said. "How about that? Hey, Chancellor, did they have *The Smurfs* in Germany?"

"Ya, but vee called zem *Die Schlümpfe*."

There was a hearty round of laughter at this. Dusty's laugh quickly transformed into another hacking fit, but this time, it was even worse than the others we had seen. His face started to turn purple as he coughed. Globs of spittle mixed with blood flew from his mouth and into the fire, making a crackling sound. E.E. began slapping him on the back to try to help him. Navy Neal stood up and admonished E.E. for slapping him, telling him that was one of the worst things you could do when someone was coughing.

Eventually, Dusty's fit tapered off, and he was reduced to a heavy wheezing. I caught Chancellor Bismarck and Navy Neal looking at each other. Their expressions told me that they knew something. Dusty got up and excused himself, saying that he needed to get some rest. E.E. left with him to make sure he made it to his tent all right.

"What's wrong with Dusty? Is he going to be okay?" I asked once I knew that Dusty couldn't hear me.

"I think it's most likely lung cancer, but it could also be tuberculosis or pneumonia," Navy Neal admitted, bowing his head. "But we have no way to test it here."

"If it's tuberculosis, then we're all fucked," Mr. Smurf blurted out. "TB is *very* contagious."

"But vee don't vant to be jumping on conclusions," Chancellor Bismarck said, oblivious to his mistake of the phrase.

"Why doesn't he go to the doctor?" Richie asked.

"*Die Schwarze Flasche*," Chancellor Bismarck said after he barked a dry laugh.

I looked at Richie, and he shrugged his shoulders, not knowing either. All three of the men sitting with us were nodding their heads solemnly.

"What does that mean?" I asked.

"It means *the black bottle*," Navy Neal translated. "It's an old hobo belief. Not *my* belief, mind you. The black bottle is believed to be a bottle of deadly poison that all hospitals have. Hoboes used to say that the last place to go when you get sick is the hospital, because the doctors and nurses will hold you down and force you to drink from the black bottle. It was believed to be a means to kill the sick and poor without having to waste money treating them. It's also believed that afterward they ship the dead bodies out to different medical colleges, where the students can practice their skills on the corpses."

The others nodded in confirmation.

Navy Neal continued, "Some hoboes like Dusty still cling to these old beliefs. If it was me, I would be in the hospital immediately, but Dusty won't listen. He's content with dying right here in his tent. Just like other hoboes before him. Most of us nowadays don't believe in all that bullshit, though. Dusty, E.E., Fat Neck Charlie, and Beef Wellington are probably all there is left of *that* sorry group."

"Has anyone tried to change his mind?" I asked. "Can't you convince him to go the hospital? I mean, how long can he last like this?"

"A number of us have tried to convince other hoboes before in similar situations," Mr. Smurf explained. "They won't listen. Dusty wouldn't listen, either. Besides, it's his choice. We don't force anything on anybody here. That is one of our rules. A man's life is his own, and that includes his death."

"In answer to your other question," Navy Neal began. "Dusty started coughing up blood even before he left here a couple of weeks ago, so this is something that he must have picked up a while back. Maybe it was when he was down in Florida a couple months ago. Looking at him now, I'd say he doesn't have much longer. He'll probably be bedridden soon."

I didn't know what to say. I felt so helpless. My intestines felt as if they were tying themselves in knots. Knowing that the man, who for all we knew probably saved our lives, was going to die—it just didn't sit right with me.

I was angry at the other hoboes for not trying harder. I was also angry at Dusty for being so stubborn. I wanted to go slap him in the face and drag him to the hospital with my own two hands, but I knew that was impossible. Based on what Navy Neal and Mr. Smurf had said, Dusty would not be swayed.

I thought back to when my grandfather had died. He had been diagnosed with esophageal cancer and had died a drawn-out death over the course of a year. He had been reduced to eating foods made in a blender at the beginning of that year. Toward the end, the doctors had installed a feeding tube in his stomach. He had given up on chemotherapy halfway through the year, as the cancer had progressed too far and the treatment wasn't worth the side effects by then.

I remembered being upset with him and my family. I didn't understand why he wouldn't keep fighting, why he wouldn't keep undergoing the chemo. And I didn't understand why my family wouldn't *make* him fight. In the end, my father had told me that it was my grandfather's choice and that it would be wrong for anyone to take that from him. When I remembered that, I understood why the other hoboes wouldn't make Dusty do anything, but it still didn't change the way I felt. There was nothing I could do.

Dusty was going to die, and soon.

*　*　*

In the morning, Dusty and the other hoboes were up early. Some of them were gone, either to the lake to bathe or off to find food or work. Dusty was sitting outside of his tent, smoking a cigarette. Richie and I joined him, lighting our own.

"I suppose y'all talked about me last night," Dusty grumbled.

I lowered my head, not answering. Richie just nodded.

"Yep, I thought so. It's all right, though. You boys need to make peace with it. I've lived a full life, and I don't have any regrets. I've done the things that I've wanted to do, and I've lived my life as free as any man can. Do you know what the difference is between a hobo and a bum?"

Richie and I shook our heads.

"A hobo works. A hobo has pride, culture, and dignity. A hobo *provides* for himself as best he can instead of waitin' for handouts and begging. Well, I suppose the best of us have been reduced to back door bummin' at one time or another, but for the most part, we provide for ourselves honestly. I'm proud to say that I've always lived like that. I have *never* been a bum."

He tapped his thumb proudly on his chest, and then he lit another cigarette and coughed again. Once he regained his composure, he carried on.

"And I have lived life by my own terms for a long time now. There are so many men out there these days that are slaves to grind, wishin' they could just pack up and go out on the open road. But I'm not knockin' anyone who wants to settle down and have a family and a steady job, don't get me wrong."

Richie and I continued to listen, not wanting to interrupt him.

"I guess what I'm tryin' to say is that there are two kinds of men. The first one is the kind that stays put. He's the kind of man that is either comfortable with the life that has been given to him and content with livin' his life on the terms that society dictates to him. Or maybe he wants to get away, but he is too chickenshit to do anythin' about it. Then, there's the kind of guy like me, runnin' free. I used to work at a big-shot office, wearin' fancy clothes. I even had a wife and daughter. Betcha didn't know that. Yep, ole Dusty Rails used to be known as Dustin James, regional manager, loving husband, and responsible father."

Dusty threw his head back and roared with laughter. Again, the laughs morphed into hacking coughs. Richie and I exchanged worried glances, but Dusty soon got it under control. He spat and then continued.

"Then my wife got up and left me for another man. Yep, the whore took another man in our bed and then told me that she's divorcin' me. That's when I decided to drop the façade that I called my life. I was tired of livin' a programmed life, if you will. I decided to say, 'Fuck the picket fence.' That's when I became a hobo. I was a little older than you, of course, but I did the same thing. I got away from it all."

I tried to imagine Dusty as a young man, but I found it very hard.

"I only had fifty dollars in my pocket when I left. I ended up hookin' up with an older hobo named Boxcar Bones and learned the ways of the Knights of the Road. Ever since then, I've held to the ways of the hobo. I've felt like a free man ever since. I've felt like I am closer to God. I have shed my life of all things unnecessary, and I only use what I need.

"There's really only *one* regret that I have. And that's leavin' my daughter, Andrea, behind. She didn't deserve that. What her mother did to me, I shouldn't have taken out on that poor little girl. That's why I was up in Virginia, where y'all met me. I knew that I'm not long for this world, so I wanted to tell her I'm sorry. And I wanted to give her the opportunity to lay into me for how I made her suffer by making her grow up without a father. But you know what? She didn't do that. She *forgave* me. I just couldn't believe it. She told me that she doesn't hate me. My daughter doesn't hate me."

He trailed off, seemingly talking to himself at this point. Tears welled up in his eyes, but he didn't cry. He just lowered his head for a moment to compose himself and then continued, "Anyway, what I'm tryin' to tell you boys is to not be sad for me. *I'm* not sad. I'm happy to have found my true callin' in life. Not many people can say that they've done that.

"I've met some colorful people since becomin' a hobo, and I love just about all of them. I've traveled north and south and east and west through this whole great country. And when I decided to make my home here in Train Town, I knew that this would be the place where I would eventually come to rest eternal."

He pointed to the woods in the distance and then resumed, "You see, I'll be buried right over there through those trees. There's a hobo cemetery through there. I didn't think it would be happenin' so soon, but it's okay with me. Like I told you already, I've lived a full life, boys. And when I die, I believe that our spirit carries on. And you can bet your ass that my spirit, like me, will also be runnin' free."

I lit another cigarette and silently contemplated his words. I supposed that there was nothing more to say on the subject. The three of us sat in silence for a while. Dusty coughed and spat blood several times throughout, but Richie and I did our best to ignore it.

As the day drew on, we got to know some of the other hoboes and the ways of "The Knights of the Road," as some of them liked to call themselves. E.E. assigned us various tasks, as it was expected of us to contribute to Train Town if we were going to stay there. Our first task was to collect firewood and stack it. Later in the day, our next task was to fill jugs of water at the mountain spring and bring them back to the camp's water supply, which was a fifty-gallon plastic drum with a cover.

Navy Neal came with us the first time to show us where the mountain spring was. That morning, he hadn't said or done anything unusual when he reapplied Neosporin and redressed my wound. I didn't need to take my pants off this time, and his hands didn't go anywhere they weren't supposed to. I kept telling myself that I was just being paranoid because of what Richie had said about him, but there was something nagging at me. It was the uncanny way Navy Neal looked at me while I was in his tent. It was almost like he was staring. I thought about saying something to Richie about it, but I didn't want to get him started again. *Maybe his eyes are bad,* I told myself. *He could have trouble focusing.*

"What does your tattoo mean? Is it something to do with the Navy?" Richie asked as we followed him to the mountain.

"In the Navy, my official capacity was a diving medical officer. Deep down, my passion has always been diving," Navy Neal explained. "The group of dolphins here are an informal Navy diver custom. They represent strength, brotherhood, and unity. The turtle is a Native American symbol of protection. And the dolphins are on his back because he is protecting them, carrying them to safety. So, I guess you could say my tattoo is a good luck talisman of sorts."

"Why are the dolphins white and the turtle red?" I asked.

"Red and white are the colors on a 'diver down' flag. But I also like red because it's the color of courage and power."

"So how did you go from being a diving medical officer to being a hobo?" Richie asked. I noticed that even though Richie was cordial with Navy Neal, he still seemed to be keeping an eye on him. He kept his distance and watched him closely.

Navy Neal stopped and turned around with an icy glare. "I don't want to be rude, kid, but that's really none of your business. I don't ask questions about other people's reasons for being here, and I demand the same respect in return."

"Sorry, man," Richie said with a red face. He took a step back, his hand creeping toward the back of his pants, where the gun was stored. I stepped in front of Richie, afraid that Navy Neal would see it and ask what he was reaching for.

"He didn't mean anything by it," I said nervously. My heart was pumping. "We're new here, and we're still learning."

"No problem, and please don't take any offense," Navy Neal smiled. The foreboding look that he had just worn while admonishing Richie quickly disappeared. "I just wanted to get that straight. We're cool now."

He turned around and continued on the path to the spring. Richie looked at me with trepidation. Reluctantly, we followed Navy Neal the rest of the way. After he showed us where the spring was, Navy Neal returned to the camp without further incident. Once we were sure that we were alone, Richie and I discussed the situation.

"What the fuck was *that* all about?" Richie said. "I told you, man. There's something about that guy. We need to get out of here."

"Hold on a minute. It's not like he punched you or anything, dude. Calm down," I said.

"Didn't you see his face? He looked crazy!"

"Now you're just overreacting. All he did was tell you to butt out of his business. You were asking too many questions."

"What's wrong with asking why he's here? He could be an escaped convict or something."

I rolled my eyes. "Yeah, and he could be Spider-Man's uncle."

"This isn't funny."

"I didn't say it was," I said. "But you know what Dusty said about hoboes. They don't talk about their old lives. It's like part of their code or something. You can't just go around asking shit like that."

Richie threw his hands up in exasperation.

"Richie, please. Listen to me. I think we should stay here."

"Are you crazy? We need to get to Mexico. They're out there looking for me!"

"Do you really think anyone is going to find you here? Why would they even look here? Think about it."

He sighed and shook his head. "You're probably right. But still, Mexico was the plan."

"Yes, that *was* the plan, but that was before we got robbed. That was before we met Dusty. Don't you care about him? Do you want to leave him to die here alone?"

"He's not alone, man. There are a bunch of people here. Besides, he should be in the hospital."

"That's not fair. He's our friend, and he helped us out, man."

Richie shrugged and then nodded. I knew that he cared about Dusty, too. He just didn't want to be close to anyone. I understood, but I didn't condone his behavior. Dusty was in our lives now. There was no changing that. He was like a grandfather to us in a way, and I didn't want to abandon him.

I thought about how Dusty had helped me to understand that there were still some good people in the world and I wanted to be one. Richie and I could selfishly walk away and leave Dusty behind, or we could stay and keep him company during his final moments. It seemed like a no-brainer to me.

We smoked cigarettes in silence for a couple of minutes, looking around at the scenery. The white rapids of the flowing mountain spring, surrounded by the lush greenery, made for a picture perfect view. Below the rapids sat a clear pool of fresh spring water that was so clear I could see the rocks at the bottom. The sound of the water rushing over the rocks, and the cool breeze blowing over the water was relaxing and quite refreshing.

"You really want to stay here?" Richie finally asked.

"I do. Honestly, man, it's the right thing to do," I said. "And besides that, I'm a little scared to go somewhere else. I think we got really lucky meeting Dusty and coming to Train Town. It could be much worse somewhere else, you know? We were stupid to think that we could just run away and find a place to live."

"But we *had* to go, man. You know that."

"I know. I'm not saying differently. I'm just saying that Dusty and E.E. and these other guys are like one big family. And they've welcomed us in like *we* are, too."

Richie nodded. "Yeah, I guess."

"And there's food and water here. And a tent, too. Do you think we'll find something like this anywhere else?"

"Probably not."

"So, will you think about it?" I asked. "For me?"

He mulled it over for a minute and then nodded and said, "Yeah, but I'm keeping my eye on Navy Neal."

We shook hands and then picked up the empty jugs to collect the water. As we worked, I stopped to observe Richie for a moment. I had always looked up to him, and I still did to some extent; however, the fact that he had killed someone and had gotten us in this mess changed things now. I was starting to think that maybe Richie wasn't always the one who knew what to do. I was comfortable with my decision to stay in Train Town. Other than going back home, I felt that it was the safest option for us. At least I *hoped* so.

PART FIVE
A NIGHTMARE TO REMEMBER

Chapter 12
THE INTERLOPERS

October 1991

Three weeks passed by. We pulled our weight around the camp as best we could, collecting firewood, fetching water, and organizing supplies. We adapted as well as we were able, integrating ourselves into their society. We got quite used to bathing in the lake and eating Mulligan Stew as well. Most of the hoboes had even begun calling us by our names instead of "boys." They warmed up to us, teaching us their ways and telling us interesting and hilarious road stories. Mr. Smurf told us that we would have to come up with hobo names pretty soon to make things official.

Two days after our confrontation with him by the spring, Navy Neal had left camp for Alabama. We overheard him telling E.E. that he had an old navy buddy in Mobile who hooked him up with medical supplies on occasion. Once he left, Richie seemed to relax more. I found that it eased my tension as well. My abrasion had healed up nicely, too. So there was no longer a need for me to visit Navy Neal's tent for Neosporin or bandages.

Dusty's condition had worsened to the point where he barely came out of his tent. Richie and I spent hours with him in there, listening to stories about his early days of catching out, the three of us doing our best to ignore that fabled "elephant" in the tent. He also taught us how to play chess on an old set he had acquired from a dump back in Virginia. Some of the pieces were missing, so we had to use substitutes. Two of the missing pawns were replaced with a bottle cap and a penny, the black knight with an acorn, and the white queen became a miniature pewter Eiffel tower.

As the days passed, the amount of time we spent in the tent with him began rapidly decreasing. We frequently ended up leaving, because he would either doze off during conversations or he would pass out from coughing too hard, both of which resulted in hours of sleep. Afterward, he would stumble out of his tent in a delirium, looking like a confused zombie, only to turn around and collapse back onto his sleeping bag.

As he got worse, he became immobilized. We had to bring him his food and water, which he barely touched. Most of the time, he was groggy and delusional; other times, he would hallucinate and yell at whatever he was seeing. There was also the *smell*. He hadn't washed himself since we had first come to Train Town, and he had begun soiling himself once he was unable to leave his tent. In the humid and unmoving Mississippi air, the smell permeated the camp. We were thankful for the occasional breeze.

It was tough to see him in such a state, but the worst was at night. The entire camp would be subjected to the horrifying lullabies of Dusty's coughing, hacking, spitting, and moaning. It was impossible to ignore.

The only distraction from Dusty at night was the music. Fat Neck Charlie strummed a beat-up old acoustic guitar that he found in an alley, and E.E. played a tarnished Marine Band harmonica. The rest of us took turns singing, making up the words as we went along. I was pleasantly surprised one night when Richie belted out a few lines about our brotherhood, even rhyming them. He had a surprisingly good voice, even impressing Chancellor Bismarck, who said that Richie would sing a good tenor. To which, Beans Mahoney teased, "Yeah, a good ten or fifteen miles away from here." This, of course, brought on a round of laughter.

During the long periods of downtime those three weeks, Richie and I managed to find a few things to occupy ourselves. Aside from our visits with Dusty, we spent countless hours swimming in the lake and wandering the woods, pretending that we were great explorers charting unknown lands. Other times we played hide and seek around the decommissioned train cars, stopping occasionally to sit in the cool shade of a rusty boxcar and smoke cigarettes.

We had been trying desperately to forget about Jim's murder and the fact that we were fugitives, but it was always there. And although Richie had relaxed considerably since we had decided to stay in Train Town, I occasionally spied him looking over his shoulder. Sometimes he would even cry in his sleep.

Chancellor Bismarck brought us into Arlington with him one day to show us around the town. As we walked around, he got the idea that begging for food and money would yield higher results with two "starving" children in tow. He was right, particularly when it came to old ladies. We cleared enough money that day to buy a couple cartons of cigarettes and a hefty amount of ingredients for Mulligan Stew.

Some of the town's residents looked at us with either suspicion or disgust, especially while we were shopping in the market. Chancellor Bismarck told us that as long as we walked around as if we belonged there, we wouldn't encounter any trouble. Unfortunately, that proved to be wrong in one situation.

A couple of hoodlums accosted Chancellor Bismarck as we were leaving the market. They shoved him back and forth, calling him a dirty bum and telling him that he shouldn't be desecrating their nice little town with his nastiness. They told him that he should have been ashamed of himself for using two young boys to do his begging. Richie told me later that he had considered pulling the gun out to scare them away, but before he could, the store owner came out to see what the commotion was. The resulting distraction enabled the three of us to slip quietly away.

When we got back to camp, E.E. admonished Chancellor Bismarck for bringing us into town. He said that we were all very lucky that someone hadn't called the police or child protective services. Chancellor Bismarck just shrugged and said, "All is vell zat ends vell."

* * *

On Thursday afternoon, E.E. was teaching Richie how to play poker. I had no interest in learning, so I decided to go down to the lake to swim. In the water, I floated around on my back, looking at the clouds, and thought about everyone back in Overture. I wondered what my parents were doing at that moment. Were they even a little bit sad about me running away? Were they trying to find me? And what about Tiffany? Did she miss me? Did she think about me when she looked at the empty chair in social studies?

I had just closed my eyes to picture her face when I heard the sudden snap of a twig breaking, followed by the rustle of leaves. *Richie must be sick of poker,* I thought.

"Finished already?" I asked, still floating on my back.

"Well, I just got here," a voice that wasn't Richie's said. I quickly opened my eyes and whirled around. I was startled by the sight of Navy Neal standing by the entrance to the woods. He was leaning up against a tree with a bottle of whiskey in his hand. He winked and said, "Hi, there."

"Oh ... N-Navy Neal," I stammered. "You scared me. I thought you were Richie."

"Oops," he said. His face was haggard, and he appeared half-drunk. He took a swig of whiskey and wiped his mouth with the back of his hand.

"Um, when did you get back from Alabama?" I asked.

"A couple minutes ago."

"Oh ... so, um, what are you doing? Are you ... uh, going to swim?"

"Huh? No, I come here to think sometimes. Go ahead with whatever you were doing, boy. Don't let me stop your fun."

"Nah, it's okay," I said. "I should probably head back to camp."

"By all means. Don't mind me."

Suddenly, I felt self-conscious. I began walking toward the shore and then hesitated. Navy Neal was standing there, staring at me, and I was about to get out of the water naked. I recalled feeling similarly the first time I had had to shower in the locker room after gym class. I had once been terrified to be seen naked by the other boys.

The prospect of being nude in front of people was embarrassing enough, but I was mostly worried that I wouldn't "measure up" to the other boys. I had told myself to stop being an idiot and gone into the shower. As it had turned out, the other boys made it a point to look anywhere *but* the private parts of their fellow classmates. With that in mind, I picked up my feet and continued walking out of the water.

"You know," Navy Neal said as I emerged from the water, "I had a young friend a while back when I was on leave. You remind me a lot of him."

"Really? Uh … cool," I said while I quickly pulled on my underwear.

"His name was Brad. Wonderful boy, but he had a big mouth."

"Huh?" I just continued dressing, unsure what to say. Was he saying that *I* had a big mouth? No, I didn't think he would say something like that. Besides, I hadn't said or done anything to warrant that distinction. I waited for him to explain himself.

"Oh, listen to me rattling on," Navy Neal said after another swig of whiskey. "It's not like *you're* Brad or anything. I don't even know why I said anything. You just kind of look like him. No big deal. Want a sip?"

He held the whiskey bottle out to me and winked. I briefly considered it, but then I shook my head and said, "No, thanks." I had taken a sip of my uncle's beer when I was nine years old. I remembered thinking it tasted like sour piss. I assumed whiskey would have tasted similar or maybe even worse. I didn't understand the adult affinity for things that tasted like ass, such as coffee, liver, and most vegetables.

"You sure?" Navy Neal asked, still offering the bottle. "It'll put hair on your chest."

"I'm all set," I said with a grin, remembering how my father used to say that to get me to eat spinach when I was little. "I, um … I should get back. I haven't checked on Dusty in while."

"Yeah, sure, kid. No problem. Hey, by the way, speaking of Dusty … as things start to progress with him, I'm here for you. If you ever need a shoulder to cry on or even just a nice big hug, ole Navy Neal is just a few tents away. Don't hesitate to come and see me."

"Thanks, that's cool."

"Don't mention it, buddy."

I nodded and left him behind to think and drink. As I traversed the trail back to the camp, I recalled how Richie had been so hard on him when we first got here. *He was so wrong,* I thought. *Navy Neal is a nice guy. He's just a little weird, that's all.* I chuckled to myself, thinking about how my judgment of character was way better than Richie's.

* * *

As I was moving past the old Yankee Flyer, I saw Fat Neck Charlie come running out of the woods across the clearing, where Dusty had first brought us to Train Town. He had left the camp two days prior to "bum for some gut-busting down at the Arlington Steel Mill to get stake for chow," which was to say, he had gone to ask for temporary work at the Arlington Steel Mill to get money for food. I stopped to watch, amused and a little curious to see him running like that, because he was usually pretty lethargic. He ran over to Beans Mahoney, and I heard him tell Beans in an urgent voice to let everyone know that there are interlopers coming.

I ran to the camp, a little worried now and forgetting all about Navy Neal. I wasn't sure what Fat Neck Charlie had meant by "interlopers," but his urgency seemed to suggest that it was something unpleasant or at least out of the ordinary. I made my way over to Richie and E.E., who were still playing poker outside of our tent.

Just as I got there, Beans Mahoney arrived to tell E.E., "Fat Neck Charlie's back. And he said that he saw some people hiking through the woods, and they're heading this way," Beans said with haste.

"Did he say how many and what type of gear they're carrying?" E.E. asked, quickly standing up.

"He said there are two of them, a man and a woman, and they look like hikers. He said they don't look like bulls or anything."

"Did they see him coming to the camp?"

"Yes, he's sure that they saw him. They weren't too far behind him. They will have also noticed the symbols and the trail leading into the camp. They'll probably be curious."

"Yes, very likely," E.E. agreed. "Let's make sure everyone knows before they get here. I'll go with you. Shelton, Richie, you two should go hide in the woods until they're gone. Quickly."

But it was futile.

Richie and I had taken about three steps toward the woods on the opposite side of the camp when a man and a woman who looked to be in their late thirties or early forties stepped into the clearing. The man had short, curly brown hair and a goatee. The woman had an attractive face and long blonde hair. They both carried large rucksacks with bedrolls and wore earth-toned hiking clothes and shoes. They glanced around curiously at the camp and spotted us immediately.

"Shit," E.E. said after a large sigh. "No point trying to hide now. Better get ready for some quick thinking boys."

"Wait, what's the big deal?" I asked, trying to hide the fright in my voice.

"Outsiders can mean trouble for a hobo camp," E.E. explained as the couple made their way toward us. "Sometimes they live and let live, but sometimes they live and make a phone call to the authorities."

Richie and I glimpsed at each other.

"What are you going to do?" Richie asked cautiously.

"We're going to do what anyone does when someone comes to your house," E.E. said. "We're going to welcome them in and be hospitable. We'll ask them to have dinner with us. Hopefully, when they see that we're not causing any trouble or doing anything more illegal than some harmless trespassing, they will leave quietly and won't cause us any grief."

With that, he walked forward to meet the newcomers. I remembered Dusty telling us when we were on the train that outsiders sometimes came and went, usually without any trouble. Still, worry had sunk its unrelenting teeth into me, and I couldn't shake it.

* * *

"Welcome to our campsite, folks. I'm Eddie. It's nice to meet you," E.E. greeted, extending his hand.

"Uh, wow, this is quite a camp," the man complimented as he shook E.E.'s hand. "I, um … I'm Michael Trachtenberg, and this is my wife, Julie."

"Nice to meet you as well, Eddie," Julie answered.

Michael and Julie curiously glanced around at the decommissioned trains and the tents. I took comfort in the fact that they seemed to be more impressed than they were concerned. As Julie scanned the camp, her eyes met mine and stopped. I saw something more heedful and quizzical than curious in her gaze, which made me anxious.

"Would you like some coffee? We can heat some up over the fire," E.E. offered.

"Sure, that sounds nice … thank you," Michael accepted. "Is that a Yankee Flyer train over there? It is? Wow, I've only seen them in pictures."

The three of them moved toward the center of the camp, E.E. leading the way. Behind E.E.'s back, Julie discreetly poked Michael with her finger and nodded toward Richie and me. He glanced at us and then back to his wife and shrugged. Richie and I looked at each other, nervous and curious.

"Have you been traveling long?" E.E. asked. At the fire pit, he scooped coffee grounds into a small pot above the fire pit and then poured water in it.

"No, actually … we just bought a house on the edge of town and decided to go hiking in our woods to see what's back here. We've only been walking for a couple of hours. We had no idea we would find a camp … or a train graveyard for that matter," Michael explained, glancing around at the camp again. "Do you all *live* here?"

His eyes darted over at Richie and me as he said that.

"Yes, most of us do," E.E. admitted, averting his eyes. "A good number of us work in the town or travel to other towns for work. We buy food and clothing as we need it, never using more than we need of anything. You could say we are minimalists, but we call ourselves hoboes."

"Hoboes? I didn't think hoboes were around anymore. I thought that way of life died out a long time ago," Michael said.

"It pretty much has, but there are a number of us who still choose to live as hoboes. We enjoy living our lives with freedom from worldly possessions, freedom from routine, and most of all, freedom from our former lives," E.E. explained. He then swept his arm out to indicate the entire camp. "This is a place where we come to start a new life, free of the judgmental eyes and the expectations of society and free of obligations and pecking orders. Every hobo here is equal and accepted as they are."

"What about *them?*" Julie asked, pointing to Richie and me with a furrowed brow. "Don't they go to school? Or do you people not believe in education?"

"Honey," Michael started in and then stopped, obviously accustomed to Julie shutting him down.

"Those are my grandkids, if you must know," E.E. claimed, lifting his chin. He convincingly sounded like a proud grandparent. "And I was a professor in my old life, so I school them myself. Worry not. They are getting a better education here than they would at any *public* school—that's for sure."

"Where are their parents?" Julie asked.

E.E. bowed his head theatrically and said "My son and his wife passed away, and these kids had nowhere else to go."

"I do apologize for my wife," Michael said, looking annoyed at Julie. "Please forgive her. We lost a son two years ago, and her concern for children—understandable as it may be—sometimes gets the better of her."

"No harm done," E.E. said, waving it away with his hand. "I'm sorry for your loss, ma'am. I surely understand what it feels like to lose a son, as I've said, although not one as young as yours must have been."

"He was only ten years old," Julie said softly. "I'm sorry for being so presumptuous."

"Already forgotten. The coffee is ready. Do you have thermos cups, or would you like to use some of our camp cups? They are clean."

"We have our own thermos cups, thank you."

"Will you be joining us for dinner? You are more than welcome, though I'm afraid we're fresh out of filet mignon."

"Oh, I am feeling a bit hungry," Michael said as he patted his belly. "And I kind of like the idea. It's not every day you get invited to have dinner with hoboes. Thanks for the offer."

Julie looked at her husband incredulously. He held her gaze defiantly, and then she looked away. *Maybe Michael isn't so whipped,* I thought and giggled to myself. Richie glanced at me sideways with a puzzled smile. I shrugged and looked back at the newcomers. I felt that our worries were unfounded and that everything would be fine with Michael and Julie. I could tell that Richie had begun to relax a little as well.

* * *

After the Trachtenbergs finished their coffee with E.E., they were properly introduced to Richie and me and the rest of the hoboes. Navy Neal had come back from the lake at one point, bottle still in hand, and he was introduced to them as well. Michael instantly took to Navy Neal. In fact, his father had also served in the Navy.

During dinner that night, Michael sat next to Navy Neal and listened intently to stories of military adventures while Julie sat next to Richie and me. She asked us several questions about life in the camp and what our learning curriculum currently consisted of. Richie did most of the talking—the *lying,* that is—because I was afraid I would somehow slip up. As we sat around the fire with full bellies, Julie became even more inquisitive.

"So, are you both comfortable living here?" she asked. "You don't ever miss living in a house, playing in a yard, or hanging out with other kids your age?"

In my peripheral vision, I saw E.E.'s eyes narrow, but he didn't say anything. Speaking for us would have seemed suspicious. I could tell that Julie was attempting to find out if we were really here by choice or not. Part of me understood, but the other part hated her for meddling.

"No, not at all. Since losing our parents, Grandpa is the only family that we have, and we *want* to be with him," Richie said. I was impressed with his wit right then. "Besides, we love living like this. We feel more in tune with mother earth, you know?" I stifled a giggle, because he was really laying it on thick now. He continued, "We don't use more than we need of anything. It seems like the best way to live, and I wouldn't have it any other way."

"Surely, you must miss going to school and being around other kids your age, though?"

"Not for a second, Mrs. Trachtenberg," Richie said in a respectful, innocent-boy tone. "Before we came here, we were terrorized at school by a bully who is our age. Then, about two days before grandpa took us here, I was in a fight with that same bully." He paused for effect and then nodded decisively. "So I can honestly say without a shadow of a doubt that I don't miss kids our age."

The sarcasm wasn't missed by Julie, nor was the closeness of truth missed by me. I recalled hearing my father telling my mother that the best lie contained a bit of truth. At the time, he had been talking about lying to keep himself out of trouble at work for some reason, but I couldn't help but wonder what my father would have thought about *this*.

Most of the other hoboes had gone back to their tents for the night, so E.E. began to douse the fire. I wasn't really tired, but I yawned theatrically while I looked at Richie. He took my hint and stood up, saying good night to Julie. As we walked away, I saw Michael get up to say good night to Navy Neal, who then stumbled off to his own tent with his bottle of whiskey. Riche and I had just about made it to our tent when Julie spoke up behind us.

"There's one thing that bothers me," she began. "How come you have a New York accent and your brother doesn't?"

Richie and I looked at each other cautiously, trying to think of an explanation. Julie sat patiently waiting for an answer, knowing that we didn't have one. Richie seemed to be at a loss, and so was E.E. for that matter. Just when I thought we were at an impasse, something came to my mind. It was a long shot, but there was no other choice.

"I was adopted," I blurted out. I tried to force out some fake tears and only succeeded in making my eyes water, but I thought that probably had a better effect anyway. It looked like I was fighting to hold my tears back. "I was adopted when I was three years old by our parents, and now they're dead. And I wish you would just stop digging into our lives like this. I don't care that Richie isn't my *blood* brother. We're brothers, and no one can change that."

Just as Richie had done, I mixed some truth in with the lie. It seemed to work, because Julie finally closed her damn mouth after she apologized profusely. I then whirled around and walked briskly to my tent without speaking a word. When Richie came in behind me, he could barely contain his laughter. He zipped up the tent and then punched me in the arm.

"That was brilliant," he said with a huge grin. "I didn't know you had it in you, Shelly."

"You think she bought it?" I asked.

"Hook, line, and sinker, my friend."

"I can't wait until they leave. It was making me so nervous the way she was looking at us. I kept thinking maybe she recognized us or something."

"Yeah, it was freaking me out, too."

"Our faces are probably on the sides of milk cartons by now, you know?" I said.

"Well, I doubt *my* face would be on any milk cartons, but *your* face would be. I'm sure your parents have probably figured out that you're with me, so they'll probably say that you were kidnapped by me, the *killer*," Richie said and then lowered his head. I could have told him that my parents knew I was with him voluntarily because of my note, but I didn't. None of that mattered anymore. He lit a cigarette and then said, "We're gonna have to figure out a way to hit the road again, you know? We've gotten too comfy here."

"I didn't think anyone would come here. I'm so sorry, Richie."

"Don't worry, man. But the quicker we get to Mexico, the better.

These people will probably rat us out when they go home. I can see it all over that Julie chick's face."

I peeked out of the tent and saw that the Trachtenbergs were still talking with E.E. *Why can't they just leave already?* I thought. *What the hell are they talking about?* I pulled my head back in the tent and said, "When they finally leave, we can ask E.E. if there are any trains that go to Mexico or at least near enough to Mexico."

"Good idea."

We fell silent, and another round of Dusty's coughing started up again. He must have woken up. His attacks were very frequent now. Even worse, every time he had them, it seemed like he would just stop breathing. We listened as Dusty moaned and coughed and hacked and spat and moaned again. I wondered what Michael and Julie would think about his sickness, too.

Richie lay down on his side of the tent and rolled over. I pulled Tiffany's note from my backpack and opened it up. Using a cigarette lighter for light, I reread her sweet proposition again. "Do u wanna maybe go out with me?" it read. I wished I had gotten the chance to answer her. It was a moot point now, but it still bothered me.

Julie Trachtenberg had hit the nail on the head for me, though. I knew Richie felt differently, but I really *did* miss home. I even missed my parents. Because I had long realized that there was nothing I could do about it now, I carefully folded Tiffany's note once again and put it away with a pang of guilt. Richie and I both fell asleep waiting for the Trachtenbergs to leave, but we were soon stirred by a commotion outside of the tent.

* * *

"This man needs to go to a hospital immediately," I heard Michael Trachtenberg yell over Dusty's moaning. Richie and I peered out of our tent and saw that he and a group of hoboes were standing outside of Dusty's tent. I saw that the sky overhead had already begun to lighten and wondered how long I had already slept. Michael continued, "He is dying. Can't you see that?"

Dusty's moans had gotten louder, and each one of his breaths was followed by a rattling sound in his throat. Fat Neck Charlie and Mr. Smurf were trying to usher Michael away from Dusty's tent, attempting to convince him that Dusty didn't want to go to a hospital, but Michael stayed. Inside the tent, E.E. was kneeling beside Dusty. We stepped out of our tent and saw Beans Mahoney standing near us.

"Is Dusty—"

"Yes," Beans bowed his head solemnly. "I think it's his time."

Richie and I joined the rest of the group around Dusty's tent. When I looked around the camp, I saw that Julie was nowhere to be found. Some of the other hoboes made their way over to Dusty's tent. Beyond them, I noticed Navy Neal leaning against a tree, empty bottle in hand, glaring at me angrily. *What the fuck?* I thought. I shuddered and quickly looked away.

"You can't just let him die here!" Michael shouted.

"It's what he wants," E.E. said simply. He noticed Richie and me standing there and motioned us over. "Dusty was calling for the two of you."

We made our way through the crowd of people and into Dusty's stench-filled tent. He was lying down on his back, breathing irregularly. His eyes were closed, and his mouth was open. His lips were cracked and covered with blood and mucus. It hurt to see him that way. We had become so close to him over the past couple of weeks. When we had first met him, despite the horrible hacking and coughing, he had seemed so full of life and so vibrant. But as he lay there now, aside from the irregular hitches in his chest and that awful rattling sound, he looked like he was already dead.

"Dusty, the boys are here with us now. Shelton and Richie are here," E.E. spoke softly to him.

He slowly opened his eyelids and tilted his head toward us. His eyes were distant and cloudy. When we moved closer, I detected a new smell emanating from him, a rotting smell. The odor made me nauseous, but I endured it for Dusty. He slowly lifted his arm and motioned for me to come close to him. I leaned in, and he put a hot, grimy hand on the back of my neck. I could feel the heat of fever rising off of him.

"Don't forget," Dusty croaked into my ear. His voice was barely

audible. I doubted that anyone else could have made out the words, except maybe Richie standing next to me. The stench of his sickly, rotting breath permeated my nostrils, and vomit threatened to surface from the bottom of my throat. I prayed that it would hold out until Dusty was finished saying what he wanted to say.

"Don't forget what?" I asked in a voice that didn't sound like my own. Tears stung at the corners of my eyes. I could tell that it took every ounce of his strength to speak these words.

"Always ... live your life ... running free," Dusty uttered. A smile touched his lips, and then he barked dry laughter until the mucus in his throat set him to coughing again. I didn't move quickly enough when he coughed, and a glob of blood-filled sputum splattered onto my cheek. I frantically wiped it off with my T-shirt. Then, my nausea got the better of me. I just barely made it out of the tent before I threw up.

Dusty died a couple hours later.

He didn't say anything else after he had spoken those last words to me. He stopped coughing and then remained still, his chest hitching and his throat rattling. Later, his chest bucked once, then twice, and finally stopped. Tears streamed down my cheeks as the life faded out of our friend. I had never watched anyone die before. It terrified me in a way. The body lying in front of us was no longer the man we knew. It was just a shell.

Numb, I walked out of the tent. Every face I saw as I passed by was somber, even Michael's. He opened his mouth as if to say something when I walked by, but then he changed his mind and closed it. Richie followed behind me in silence. When he opened our tent for me, I realized I could still smell Dusty in my nose.

"Are you okay, man?" he asked.

"Yeah, I guess," I murmured. "We knew he was going to die for a while now, but it's still hard, you know?"

"Yeah, I know," Richie said gravely.

I put my head in my hands and cried hard. Richie put his arm around me and held me for a few minutes. I think he cried, too, but I wasn't sure. I was wrapped in my own blanket of grief. I cried for everything: Dusty, my parents, this whole fucking trip. I wanted to go home, but I couldn't. I wanted Richie to tell me that we should go back home, but he wouldn't. I wanted Dusty to be alive, but he wasn't. I felt like nothing was as it should have been.

"Did you see Julie anywhere?" I said through my hands.

"No, I didn't. Do you think she went to get help? If she did, then we'll need to hide if anyone comes … or maybe we should just leave right now."

I didn't know what to say or do. I just knew that I felt filthy. Dusty had touched my neck with his sweaty, dying hand and had coughed that stuff on my face. I knew it wasn't his fault, but the memory of it made me nauseous all over again. The lingering smell of him, whether it was all in my head or not, and the smell of my vomit on my breath was too just much to handle.

"Whatever you decide, Richie," I said. "I don't know anything anymore. I'm gonna go wash up in the lake, okay?"

"Yeah," he said softly. "Take your time. I'll pack everything up, and then I'll go talk to E.E. and see if he knows if there are any trains to Mexico."

I ducked out of the tent and quietly made my way down to the lake, unaware that Navy Neal was following me.

Chapter 13
VIRTUTE ET ARMIS

October 1991

Daylight was approaching as I walked down the trail to the lake. I undressed in silence and waded into the water. My thoughts were racing through my brain as fresh tears ran down my face. Dusty was dead, and we would be on the move again tomorrow or maybe even today after Dusty's burial.

I thought back to John's funeral. It took place two days after he had died, and I remembered seeing so many people there, so many sad faces surrounded in a sea of black clothing. There were a lot of people I didn't even know. There were friends of John's, friends and co-workers of my parents, people from the town's church, and even some of John's teachers from school. It was one of the saddest days of my life, but as they lowered his coffin down into the cold ground, I looked around at everyone and felt a tinge of pride. All of these people were here for my big brother, John.

Dusty's funeral would be much smaller compared to John's. There would only be a handful of hoboes, along with Richie and me. *If we are still here when they bury him,* I told myself. As I washed, I thought I saw movement in the woods, but I dismissed it after a moment. I dunked my head under the water to wash Dusty off of me. I tried to wash my tears away as well. I scrubbed hard at my eyes under the water. I scrubbed until they hurt. Then I heard the sounds of someone approaching.

I emerged from the water to see Navy Neal on the shore. His eyes were glossed over, and he wore a devilish grin. He began taking his clothes off, preparing to get in the water with me.

"Hi there, twink," he said.

"W-what are you doing?" I asked nervously. My heart was pounding. The way he was looking at me earlier before I went into Dusty's tent had freaked me out. I hadn't had time to process it right then and there, but now that he was in front of me, I recalled just how crazy his eyes were. And he looked just the same now.

"I'm coming in for a swim. Want some company?" he asked. He removed the last piece of clothing and waded into the water.

"Um, I don't know. I should really—"

"Aw, come on, kid. I could sure use some company. I'm real upset about Dusty."

He waded over to me. Something told me I should run. He was creeping me out. When he spoke, his voice even sounded weird. It sounded breathy and uneasy. I moved to get past him, and he put his arm out to stop me.

"Where you going, kid?"

"I just wanna go, please," I said, almost begging. My heart was racing now. I was very scared.

"You know," he said, wrapping his arm tightly around my chest and moving in behind me. "Brad was a big mouth. I lost everything because of that kid. He wasn't supposed to tell anyone. But you're not a big mouth, are you, Shelton?"

He was breathing heavily now. Cold fear and panic rapidly spread through me. I felt like I couldn't breathe. I had never in my life been in a fight, and Navy Neal was much bigger than I was. I didn't know what to say or do. I prayed that he would just let me go.

I felt his hand move around toward my crotch, and he cupped me there. He whispered in my ear, "Yeah, you like that. Don't you, my little twink?" My nerves fluttered in sheer panic. I couldn't move because of his arm across my chest. He was too strong. I looked down at the tattoo on his forearm, and the moving muscles made it look like the dolphins were actually swimming.

Then, as he was fondling me, he let out a sigh of pleasure, and the arm across my chest loosened a bit. I recognized that as a window of opportunity. I slid down into the water out from under his grasp and then sprang forward as hard as I could. I felt his hands grabbing for me as I tried to swim away. He soon seized my ankle, pulling me back toward him. I shot out of the water, unable to hold my breath for long in such a panic.

As I wiped the water from my eyes, I tried to get past him, but he caught me by the hair. I yelped as he yanked me back. I twisted around and swung at him, broadly missing. He grinned widely and punched me in the jaw. Bursts of light spread across my vision, and I went sprawling into the water, losing consciousness for a split second. When I clawed my way back up, swallowing a bunch of water in the process, I quickly resurfaced and tried to run again.

He yanked on my hair again and pulled me into him. As he covered my mouth with one hand, he told me that it would hurt less if I stopped fighting. Dread overcame me, and I bit his finger, causing him to yell out. I tried to struggle free, but he was just too strong. He moved his arm down and closed it around my neck, cutting off my air supply.

"Don't say a word, boy," he said. "You don't want the Trachtenbergs to hear you and then cause more trouble for us, do you? Just shut your fucking mouth and let this happen."

From the corner of my eye, I could still see his tattoo. The dolphins and the turtle seemed to mock me as he squeezed my neck.

"I can't wait anymore. I've been watching you. Watching and waiting for the perfect opportunity. Mmm, you're gonna love this, twink."

Behind me, he was grinding himself against me under the water. I could feel him getting hard. I tried bringing my leg up to kick him in the balls, but the weight of the water made my kick slow and sluggish. And he was ready for me. He turned as I kicked, and my leg gingerly connected with his thigh.

He laughed in my ear and told me he was going to love breaking my little cherry. My knees grew weak as he squeezed his arm tighter around my throat. His other hand cupped around my crotch again, and I felt his hardness trying to force its way into me from behind. I squeezed my eyes shut in horrific anticipation, hoping that I would pass out before I felt anything. Then I heard Richie yell.

"Get the fuck away from him," he roared.

Navy Neal wheeled around, releasing me in his surprise. As I choked on the air rushing back into my lungs, I heard Navy Neal gasp behind me. I turned and saw Richie standing on the shore, feet planted in the shallow water, the gun gripped in both of his hands. He had a murderous look on his face that chilled me to the bone.

"Take it easy, boy," Navy Neal said with a tremble in his voice. He had his hands raised, and he began walking toward Richie. "I wasn't going to hurt him. We were just playing around."

"Don't come any closer to me," Richie said so low that I barely heard it. The gun was wobbling in his shaky hands, but he kept it trained on Navy Neal. "I'll shoot you, Jim. I swear it."

Navy Neal stopped for a second. "Jim? Who is Jim? Are you okay, kid?"

"Shelly, get out of the water. Put your clothes on," Richie said.

Until then, I had been frozen in place, but his words got me moving. I took a few steps, moving in an arc away from Navy Neal. As Richie watched me, Navy Neal began quickly moving toward the shore again. He was closing in on Richie fast. When Navy Neal was within arm's reach, Richie screamed and then squeezed the trigger.

Three loud gunshots thundered through the still morning air, deafening me. Overhead, a flock of birds was rousted from their slumber and flew from one side of the trees to another. Navy Neal jerked back with each shot and fell backward. I screamed and then urinated in fright as his body hit the water with a big splash.

A few feet away from me, the lifeless corpse floated face-up. His eyes and mouth were open in an expression of shock. There were three gruesome red holes in his chest, and a crimson cloud was rapidly spreading in the water around him. I looked from the corpse to Richie. He was still standing the same way, the gun pointed in the same direction. Tendrils of smoke curled in the air, wafting from the barrel of the gun.

I looked back at the body and saw that it was drifting slowly toward me. Terrified that the body would touch me, I sprang into action and sprinted to the shore. When I got to Richie, his hands were at his sides, one of them still shakily clutching the gun. Tears streamed down his face as he stared at Navy Neal's body.

"Oh, my God, Richie! What did you do? What the fuck did you do?" I yelled. I dropped to my knees in front of him, feeling somewhat awkward because of my naked body but not caring. I couldn't believe my best friend—no, my brother—had just killed *another* person. I didn't know what to think or how to feel. My brain held a traffic jam of thoughts.

"Put your clothes on, Shelly. We have to go," Richie said flatly, without looking at me. He was still staring at the body of Navy Neal.

As I dressed frantically, E.E., Fat Neck Charlie, Mr. Smurf, and Chancellor Bismarck all appeared from the woods, Michael Trachtenberg leading the charge. Michael jerked his head back and forth wildly, scanning the area. The hoboes moved in around him cautiously.

"Were those gunshots?" Michael asked us. "What ... oh, my God. Is that a dead body?"

"It's Navy Neal," Richie muttered. He spoke slowly, as if he had been drugged. His eyes still remained locked on the body in the water. "He tried to rape Shelly, and I killed him. I killed the bastard dead."

"What the hell is going on here? What is *wrong* with you people?" Michael said. "What the hell kind of a place is this? People dying in tents, people raping kids, people *shooting* people? Practically in our own backyard, for heaven's sake! This is ... this is a horrible place!" Michael bellowed, yet everyone ignored him.

E.E. and Mr. Smurf quietly waded into the water and dragged Navy Neal's body to the shore and laid him on his back. His mouth had partially closed, and blood and water now seeped from the bullet holes in his chest. Mr. Smurf checked for a pulse and then looked at E.E. and shook his head. Navy Neal was definitely dead. Michael then began pacing back and forth.

The hoboes stood there silently, their heads bowed. Two of their own had died today, and an outsider had seen the whole thing. It couldn't get much worse for them. E.E. gazed out at the lake, knowing that this would most likely mean the end of Train Town. As Michael continued to frantically babble and pace back and forth, the other hoboes stood over Navy Neal's body and discussed the situation.

Richie spoke up beside me. "He was gonna hurt you, Shelly ... he was gonna *hurt* you. I had to do it. I had to."

"I know, Richie. I'm glad you did it. You saved me, man." I said. Despite my horror, I felt I owed it to him to tell him that. I hated to think how things would have been if he hadn't shown up.

The hoboes on the beach glanced at us periodically as they talked to each other. They had expressions of dismay on their faces. I could tell that they no longer viewed us as family. To them, we were now the same as the Trachtenbergs. We were outsiders once again.

Richie turned toward me with a haunted look in his tearful eyes. He dropped to his knees in the sand and spoke slowly. "He raped me, Shelly. I should have told you earlier, but I just couldn't."

My jaw dropped open in shock, and I looked over at Navy Neal in disbelief.

"Not him. I'm talking about Jim. That's why I killed him, Shelly."

"Richie, I ... I don't know what to say," I stammered. I put my hand on his shoulder and crouched down next to him.

He began by telling me about Jim's visits to his bedroom some nights. He confided how helpless he had felt as Jim violated him, how sometimes he would try to fight back and would just be beaten for it, how he had cried more tears than he had thought a human could cry every time Jim had finished with him, how ashamed he had felt of himself, how he had sometimes even thought about killing himself.

He told me that Jim had taken something away from his soul, something that could never be replaced.

As he spoke, I said nothing, even though I had a million questions. I knew that if I were to interrupt him, he might not have finished. He just needed to tell me everything at once and get it all out of him. The truth had been festering within him for a long time now, eating away at him from the inside. I didn't know how he had been able to keep that bottled up for so long. Even just *hearing* about it made me feel like puking and crying at the same time.

He cried as he told me about the sick things that Jim had done to him, but I had an idea that these were tears of relief, because it was finally over and because he could finally talk about it with someone. He explained that the story he had told me on the highway about the day he had killed Jim had all been true except for one part. When Jim had Richie pinned against the bathroom sink with his face pressed against the mirror, Jim hadn't been choking Richie. He had been attempting to rape him again.

While Richie was telling me this, Chancellor Bismarck and Mr. Smurf picked Navy Neal up under the arms and began dragging him back to the camp. I watched as his dangling feet carved two lines in the sand behind them. E.E. and Fat Neck Charlie were trying to calm Michael down and get him back to the camp, but he was still ranting and pacing. I knew that it was important for Richie to get all of this off of his chest, but I could feel time slipping away from us.

"Richie, I'm sorry, but we have to go," I said. I had to try to take control of the situation. "We need to leave before anyone shows up. If Julie went for help, then they could be here any minute."

"We need to get our bags," he said as he wiped his eyes and composed himself. We stood up and headed toward the trail leading back to camp.

"Where are you two going? You're not going anywhere! You just killed somebody!" Michael yelled from behind us.

Richie turned around and pointed the gun at Michael. Alarm momentarily seized me, but then I remembered that Richie had said there had only been three bullets in the gun—three bullets, three shots, three holes in Navy Neal's back. Richie was bluffing. The gun was empty, but Michael didn't know that. He winced, put his hands in front of his face, and begged Richie not to shoot him. I felt

sympathy for Michael as I watched the crotch of his khakis darken
with urine.

* * *

We scuttled up the path and back to the camp, leaving the
terrified Michael Trachtenberg behind us. Just as we made it to our
tent, Julie appeared from the woods with two EMTs and a police
officer. Seeing that uniform with the shiny badge and holstered
pistol made my nerves flutter. Chancellor Bismarck and Mr. Smurf
were still dragging Navy Neal's body, but they dropped it as soon as
they saw the cop. Luckily, the officer hadn't seen them dragging the
body, and when they dropped it, it was hidden from obvious view
by a large patch of overgrowth. The cop didn't have his gun drawn
either, so he somehow must not have heard the shots earlier.

A stroke of luck, I thought.

I saw Julie pointing over at Dusty's tent, and the EMTs rushed
in to investigate while the police officer questioned the surrounding
hoboes. We took advantage of being undetected and snuck over
to our tent. E.E. rushed over to talk with the cop. As we hastily
collected our belongings, we overheard snippets of the conversation
outside.

"… have the right to not go to the hospital …"

"… is private property … must have a fire permit for a fire this
size in the woods …"

"… is dead … what is the John Doe's name …"

"… don't know his real name …"

"… reports of possible runaways living in this camp …"

We slung our packed bags over our shoulders, and then Richie
poked his head out of the tent. The cop had his back to us, so we
quietly exited the tent and crept toward the woods. I saw Richie
pull the gun out of his waistband as he kept his eyes on the cop. Just
then, Michael came darting past the Yankee Flyer, glancing wildly
around. When he saw the officer, he began waving his arms around
and pointing at Richie.

*"Officer! Officer! That boy there just shot and killed a man! A-and then
he pointed his gun at me!"* he screamed.

The policeman wheeled around and spotted Michael gesturing wildly and then followed Michael's gaze to us. The confused officer raised his arm up and told us to stop right there. He began walking toward us, and Richie leveled the gun at him. The cop froze and put his hands up.

"Now there's no need for that, son. Let's just calm down. Please put the gun down," the officer coaxed. "Let's just talk things over. I'm sure there is a good explanation for everything."

"Oh, my God, now he's pulling the gun on *you!*" Michael shrieked in a panicky voice. "This kid is a psycho, officer. You have to do something!"

"Sir, I am handling the situation now. Please, everyone just calm down," the officer suggested.

"You're not taking me away," Richie said shakily. His eyes were panic-stricken like an antelope about to be caught by a lion.

"Please, son, no one is taking you anywhere just yet. Let's just put the gun down, and we'll talk about it. You're only making things worse. There is a peaceful way to resolve things."

"Fuck you!" Richie spat, firming his grip on the gun. "You're not gonna get in my head. I've seen the movies. You're gonna try to talk me down, get the gun away from me, and then jump on me. I'm not stupid. And you're not Clint Eastwood."

I stood in silent disbelief next to Richie. My eyes met the cop's eyes at one point, and I quickly looked away. Feelings of hopelessness and despair washed over me, compiling my terror. I didn't think there was any way out of this. The gun wasn't even loaded. The only leverage Richie had was that the cop didn't know it.

"Son, you've got it all wrong. This is real life. This isn't the movies. If what this man says is true, if you have killed a man, then yes, there will be consequences. But those consequences will be much worse if you shoot a police officer." He spoke calmly and deliberately, maintaining eye contact with Richie. As he continued to hold his arms up, he quickly looked around the area. After seeing the train cars, he turned his attention to Richie again. "You see, consequences are like a train, son. Each one is connected to the next. You kill someone, there are consequences. You kill another person to avoid those consequences, and there are just more attached to that. The only way you can stop the train is to get off of it. That starts with putting the gun down, okay?"

Richie continued to point the gun at the officer. He frantically glanced around, thinking about what to do next.

"I can *help* you, son," the cop said. "I *want* to help you, but I can't do that with a gun pointed in my face. What's your name, son? My name's Chris."

"I don't care what your name is! You don't give a shit about me! Where were you guys when Navy Neal attacked Shelly? Huh? Where were you when Jim was beating me and my mother? Where were you when he ... when he—" Richie's voice wavered as he fought back the tears. "Where the fuck were you when he tried to *kill* me?" As he spoke, his face grew redder, and he jerked the gun forward with each word. "You don't give a shit. You're just gonna put me in some jail. And everyone knows what happens *there*. No way! No fucking way!"

The cop furrowed his eyebrows while Richie spoke, not fully understanding what was being said. He then tried another approach. He looked me in the eye and asked, "Are you Shelly? I heard him calling you Shelly."

"*Don't fucking talk to him!*" Richie screamed, tears gushing from his eyes. "*He hasn't done anything! Shelly's a good person. He's not like me!*"

"Okay, son, I apologize. Let's just keep things peaceful."

"I'm not your fucking son! Stop calling me that."

"Richie, maybe you should just give yourself up," E.E. chimed in. "This really is making things worse."

I had forgotten that everyone else was standing around us. All of the hoboes and the EMTs were silently watching. Michael was still standing over by the Yankee Flyer, but he had taken a few steps forward. Julie was carefully working her way over to him, too. Richie wavered momentarily, first looking to E.E. and then to Michael and Julie. I saw in his eyes that he wanted to believe that everything would be okay. Then, as Richie's eyes were averted, the cop took two sly steps toward us. Richie snapped his head back and screamed at him.

"*Get the fuck away from me!*" he yelled. "*Get down! Get down on the ground right now!*"

"Okay, Richie," the cop said as he lowered himself onto his knees. "I just want you to talk to me without the gun. What can I do to get you to drop the gun and talk about this without further violence?"

"You can get down on the ground and stay there. Me and Shelly are leaving, and you're not gonna stop us."

"Where are you going to go, Richie? You don't really want to keep running, do you? What about your friend Shelly there? Do you want him to have to keep running?"

I saw hesitation in Richie's eyes just then. The cop saw it, too. Richie lowered the gun ever-so-slightly, so slight that I may have been the only one to notice, except for maybe the cop. Then, Richie's eyes narrowed, and he put both hands on the gun, firmly training it on the officer once again.

"Not so fast, you fuckin' asshole," Richie said to the cop. "You almost had me there, but I know now that you're just waiting, just waiting for your opportunity. You don't care about Shelly, and you don't care about me!"

"That's not true," the cop interjected.

"Yeah, right … if I drop the gun, you'd be right on top of me, beating me up. That's what cops do. My father told me that before he got sent up. So you're no better than Jim. You prey on people. You took my father away from us!"

"I don't know your father, Richie," the cop said plainly. He looked like he was losing patience. "I just want you to drop the gun before you do anything stupid."

"The only thing that would be stupid is to give in to you and let you take us away," Richie said. "Lie down on your stomach and put your hands behind your head. Yeah, there you go. How does it feel for *you?*"

When the cop was on the ground with his hands interlocked behind his head, Richie opened his mouth to say something to me.

Just then, Julie tripped over Navy Neal's body in the overgrowth on her way over to Michael. She put her hands up to her mouth and shrieked. Once Richie looked away, the cop sprang up to take Richie down. I saw what was happening and screamed for Richie to watch out.

Only seconds passed then, but it felt much longer, an eternity almost.

Richie whipped his head around and squeezed the trigger of the pistol involuntarily. The thundering clap of a gunshot pierced through the air, rupturing my eardrum. As the pain in my ear seared through my head, the cop was thrown backward from the force of the bullet and crashed onto the ground. Richie stared gape-mouthed at the downed police officer, who was screaming in pain and holding his shoulder with a bloody hand.

"Oh, my God, Shelly! There were only three bullets in the clip, I know it! I must have … I must have counted wrong, but how could I have?" Richie ranted almost incoherently. "I pulled the clip out, and I counted three bullets. I *know* it! Oh, my god, what are we gonna do, Shelly?"

As I tried to ignore the droning pain in my ear, I closed my eyes and told myself not to panic. I considered the situation. The cop was still alive. That was a good thing, one less mark against Richie. But shooting a police officer, according to what I had heard from my father, was considered a crime worse than shooting God. There was no chance for Richie now. We had to run. That was the only solution I could think of. If we could get away from here and somehow make it to Mexico, they wouldn't be able touch us then.

Suddenly, a voice came over the officer's radio, inquiring about the gunshot. The cop pressed the button on his radio and yelled at the voice, "Hold positions and call for backup". The voice acknowledged and announced that backup was already en route. Richie, who was deep in thought, seemed not to notice.

"Richie, we have to run," I urged impatiently. "We have to run, now!"

"Why did you make me do this?" Richie screamed to the police officer writhing on the ground. He jerked the gun toward the cop. "Why couldn't you have just let us go?"

The cop just glared at Richie, his teeth gritted, holding his shoulder and breathing heavily. Several beads of sweat had formed on his forehead. He was trying to overcome the pain. Through his initial screams of pain, the officer had obviously not heard what Richie had said about the bullets in the gun.

"Let's go, Richie. We have to go," I urged, pulling his shirt as I began to run. "There are other cops out there, and they heard the gunshot, man. They called in backup. We have to go."

I was surprised and a little scared at my composure, but I knew I had to be strong. Richie followed me as I sprinted toward the trees. Behind us, I could hear the cop yelling at us to stop. The EMTs quickly made their way over to him to examine his gunshot wound.

As we made it to the woods, I heard him yelling into his radio. He gave our descriptions and warned the other officers in the area. "I repeat, hold your positions. Do *not* enter the woods. They are coming straight to you! They are headed toward the train tracks, and one of them is armed and dangerous. I repeat, one of them is armed and dangerous."

Despite what the cop had said, we kept running. We didn't have any other choice. I held on to the hope that we would come out on the tracks away from where the police were positioned.

* * *

As we ran through the woods, we heard sirens approaching. It was hard to tell exactly how far away the sirens were, but one thing became painfully clear: the police station must have been pretty fucking close for them to arrive here so soon.

Richie was ahead of me now. Several times, branches that he moved out of his way whipped me in the face. I just prayed that I wouldn't get hit in the eyes. He stopped running and looked around frantically, considering an alternate route. Then he shook his head and began running again. I followed, hoping for a miracle.

After we passed an overturned antique handcar, we finally made it to the train tracks. We saw that there were two Rhino 660 off-road police vehicles and an ambulance parked on the train tracks. Then we noticed two police cars speeding along the rails toward us, their sirens wailing and lights flashing. Richie dove to the ground and crawled back behind the overturned handcar. I followed his example and leaned up against the handcar with him. My heart thundered in my chest. The whole thing felt so surreal.

We heard the sirens switch off and the doors of the police cruisers open and close. I thought that maybe no one had spotted us coming out of the woods because of the approaching police cars, but then a police officer shouted through a megaphone in our direction, "*This is the Mississippi Highway Patrol. Drop your weapon and come out with your hands up.*"

"Fuck, fuck, fuck!" Richie yelled.

"What are we gonna do?" I asked, my voice cracking in panic.

"I don't know, Shelly. I don't know."

Richie was panicking as much as I was. Beads of sweat peppered his forehead. As he breathed heavily, he gripped the gun in his hand and bumped the sides of his fists against his temples in frustration. He was psyching himself up. I didn't like the look on his face. His eyes looked desperate and crazy. As the officer behind the police vehicle shouted again, I saw Richie's face suddenly harden and become much calmer.

"Maybe we should just turn ourselves in," I pleaded, sensing that he was thinking irrationally. "With Jim, it was self-defense, and with Navy Neal, you were saving me, so maybe it won't be so bad."

"I don't think I can do that, Shelly," Richie said calmly. His breathing had slowed and become more focused. "I've killed two people and sent a kid to the hospital, not to mention I just shot a fucking cop. They won't go easy on me." He cradled the gun in his hands and stared at it. He had begun to cry again. "I can't go to jail. I just can't. What if someone does the same thing to me that Jim did? That happens in prisons all the time." He shook his head. "No way. I would rather die than to have that happen. It's over for me, Shelly. It's over."

"What do you mean it's over?"

"We have you surrounded. This is your final warning. Put your weapon down and come out with your hands up," the megaphone blared again.

"I mean just what I said. You'll be fine, Shelly. They'll take you back home. You haven't done anything wrong, okay? Things will be okay for you, but they will never be okay for me. I know that now," Richie said and sighed heavily. "I was fooling myself. I tried ... I tried and I failed, and now there's nothing left to do. There's no escape."

He peeked over the top of the handcar and then continued, "I want to believe you, Shelly. I *need* to believe that things won't go so bad for me, that they will consider the self-defense part of it, but I just don't know. I'm afraid to take that chance, man. I just don't know for sure."

He lowered his head for a moment and then looked me in the eyes. Incredibly, he smiled at me. He said, "What I *do* know is that there's no more time to think. I can't be scared anymore. It's time for me to act. It's time for me to end this, Shelly." Tears streamed down his cheeks, making streaks in the dirt on his face. As I swallowed a lump in my throat, I fought back my own tears.

Richie wiped his tears away, looked down at the gun in his hands, and said, "It's just like that cop said. This is the final stop on the train of consequences."

He sees that there's no other way, I thought. *He's going to follow the cop's advice and turn himself in. It will be hard, seeing them take him away, but we'll get through it. Things will eventually be okay. They will go easy on him because of what he's been through. Everything he did was in self-defense. And shooting the cop was an accident. He will probably get sentenced to juvie for a couple years, but then we can move on with our lives. I need to let him know that he's doing the right thing.*

"It's okay, Richie. I think it's the right thing to do," I told him and then hugged him.

He clutched me tightly and spoke in my ear, "Just remember me, Shelly. I love you, man. Don't ever forget me."

He let go of me and stood up, gun grasped tightly in his hand. The weight of his words suddenly hit me. I sprang up when I realized his true intentions. I was momentarily distracted when I saw the blur of gray uniforms and black uniforms, all with shiny badges, and the muzzles of rifles and pistols all pointed in our direction. In what seemed like slow motion to me, I saw Richie raise his arm up, the empty gun in hand.

I felt the blood rushing from my face and ice creeping into my veins. I tried to scream, "There are no bullets in the gun," but nothing came out. Richie squeezed his eyes shut in anticipation as he brought the gun up and pointed it at the police. I watched as his body jerked back several times and I saw specks of blood and T-shirt flying out of his back.

Then, I heard the shots, so many thundering shots.

The police peppered my best friend with bullets, and he fell backward onto the ground, dead. I then heard someone yelling, "Hold your fire, goddamn it!" I let out a scream and scrambled over to him, holding his lifeless body in my arms. One of his eyes was open and partly rolled up into the eyelid. A grimace of pain was frozen onto his face. I cried out and held him in my arms, rocking him back and forth. My best friend was dead.

* * *

I was only vaguely aware of everything that followed. As I moaned and wailed, embracing Richie's lifeless body, several policemen moved in to retrieve the gun. I heard one of them say that there were no bullets in it, and then a hush fell over them. I could feel their eyes on me, knowing that I had heard, but I didn't care. Richie was dead, and there was nothing else.

They pried me away from Richie's body at one point. When they hoisted me up, their hands hooked under my armpits, I looked down at my hands covered in Richie's blood. The sight of it made my head swim, and I felt like vomiting. The policemen sat me down on the rail of the train tracks, and two of them stayed with me, attempting to ask me questions. I didn't speak. I only stared over at Richie's body.

I saw E.E., Mr. Smurf, Chuck Norris, Chancellor Bismarck, and Beans Mahoney being escorted out of the woods in handcuffs. They

184

were all silent and solemn except for Chancellor Bismarck, who was yelling obscenities in German. Fat Neck Charlie must have gotten away in the confusion, and Beef Wellington was out bumming around for food in Arlington.

The interlopers, Michael and Julie Trachtenberg, came traipsing out of the woods later and looked quite proud of themselves, because they had "done something good." I listened as they gave their statements to the police. The way things sounded coming from their mouths, Richie and I were practically being brainwashed and subjected to unspeakable things.

Julie glanced over at me with an exaggerated sympathy, making sure that the police could see, and then told them that she just wished they could have gotten here sooner to prevent this horrible tragedy. I understood how things must have looked, but part of me wanted to grab one of the cops' guns and shoot both of the Trachtenbergs in the face for the trouble they had caused. But I didn't have the strength for that. Instead, I just stared at Richie, who was still on the ground where he had fallen, slowly changing color.

Several more police vehicles and another ambulance appeared later on, splashing blue and red lights all over my friend's dead body. After the coroner showed up and looked over the bodies, they finally covered Richie. When they did, a stinging feeling pierced my heart. That would be the last time I would ever see his face.

* * *

I was soon shipped to the police station, and the officers sat me in a dirty room with only a table, two chairs, a video camera in the corner, and a large mirrored wall. A large man in a gray uniform later came in and sat in the chair across from me. He had red hair and a gaggle of freckles on his face that made him look like he had walked into a spray of chocolate. He said his name was Officer Kirk Boucher. He told me he knew that I hadn't done anything wrong. He just wanted to know my name and where to contact my parents.

I told him my name, and everything that had happened to us. I let it all out, stopping only to clear my throat. Throughout my testimony, I repeatedly emphasized that Richie had only been defending me. He had *saved* me. I also told him of Richie's past and how he had been traumatized by the police arresting his father when he was just a little boy. I told him everything about Jim, too.

The officer didn't seem to care about any of it. He listened patiently and emotionlessly, occasionally writing down some of the things I said. A couple of times, he glanced up at the camera in the corner. While I spoke, I couldn't look him in the eyes. I focused mainly on the patch on the shoulder of his uniform, which read, "Mississippi Highway Patrol." At the center of the patch was an eagle, and beneath that was a Latin phrase, *"Virtute et armis."* As I tried not to think about the future, I pondered its meaning while the officer reviewed his notes.

"So you said he had counted only three bullets in the magazine?" Officer Boucher inquired when he finished reading.

"Yes, and I believe him," I said. "If you would have seen his face, you would have, too. He was totally surprised when the gun went off. I was, too."

"He most likely didn't account for the bullet in the chamber," Officer Boucher said as he closed the case folder and stood up. "This is a prime example of why children shouldn't have access to firearms."

"What happened to that cop? Is he in the hospital?" I asked.

"Yes, he is. He will be okay, though. There was minimal nerve damage and blood loss. I might add that he is a fine police officer and it's a damn shame that he will be out of work for so long. But at least he survived. I would hate to have told his wife and kids if he didn't."

He eyed me accusingly, as if *I* had been the one who had pulled the trigger. Then, he sighed and walked out of the room. I rested my chin on my arms and closed my eyes. Although I didn't wish the wounded officer any harm, I couldn't bring myself to feel bad for him. My brother had just died—the second one in a less than a year.

* * *

Sometime after Officer Boucher left the room, I went to the

restroom. I stood in front of the mirror and looked at myself for the first time in almost a month. My face was pale and gaunt, and there were dark circles under my bloodshot eyes. I looked ten years older. There was a streak of crusted blood that ran from my ear down to my chin. I had forgotten all about my ruptured eardrum, which had subsided to a dull throb every now and then. The gun had been mere inches from my face when it had gone off.

I kept replaying the scenes in my head—the look of surprise on Richie's face when the gun had gone off and he had shot that cop, the eerie way he had smiled just moments before he had stood up and raised the empty pistol, the disturbing way his body had jerked back from the force of the bullets. But mostly, my mind kept flashing back to the expression of anguish on his dead face.

I couldn't believe he was gone. He wouldn't laugh anymore. He wouldn't make *me* laugh anymore. He was never coming back. Just like John. *Why did this have to happen?* I asked God. *It's bad enough that you took John from me. Why did you have to take Richie, too? It's not fair!*

Fresh tears rolled down my cheeks. I didn't think I would be able to cry anymore, but I was wrong. It was overwhelming to think about how much death I had seen in just one day. Navy Neal, Dusty, and Richie had all died right in front of me.

Death is attracted to me, I thought with a shudder.

A police officer came into the restroom then and went into one of the stalls. I splashed water on my face and shuffled over to the urinal to pee. As I was taking care of business, I heard a loud, echoing fart come from the cop's stall, and I had to stifle a giggle. It reminded me of the one Richie had touched off in Jim's car on the way down here. I didn't think it was possible to laugh and cry at the same time, but wonders never ceased. I supposed a bit of gas and the right acoustics could lighten even the darkest of moods.

* * *

Naturally, Officer Boucher had called my parents, and they immediately booked a flight to Mississippi to come and get me. I dreaded their arrival as I waited in the police station. I imagined that they would burst in and wag their fingers in my face, telling me that they had more important things to deal with, that I had delayed their divorce long enough. They would tell me that I had caused them more stress than I was worth, that I would be grounded for life, and that I would have to sit in my room and never again see the light of day for as long as I lived.

However, when my mother and father pushed open the door to the police station, they didn't say or do any of that. They saw me sitting there, and they both burst out into tears. The sight of them made me cry as well. I hadn't realized until that moment just how much I had immensely missed them. They hurried over to me and hugged me so tightly that I could barely breathe, but I didn't mind.

"Oh, my baby boy," my mother said, sniffling and squeezing me tightly. "We love you so very much. Thank God you're safe."

"We were so scared. We thought we lost you," my father said.

My mother gently took my face between her hands and looked me in the eyes. I noticed dark circles under her bloodshot eyes. She said, "The police told us everything. Are you okay?"

I tried to answer, but I was overwhelmed and I started crying even harder. I could barely breathe through my sobs. I felt like I was three years old again, unable to control my emotions. My mother put my head against her shoulder and stroked the back of my head. I could feel my father's hand on my shoulder, too. Their touches soothed me. After a couple of minutes, I finally calmed down.

"Are you mad at me?" I managed to ask.

"You had us very worried, Shelton," my father said. "We haven't really slept the whole time you were gone. Your mother hasn't been eating. We haven't even gone into work. We've been on the phone every day, hanging up posters, trying to find you."

"But that's behind us now," my mother said. She looked at my father with raised eyebrows.

"Yes. Yes it is," my father said. "We're just happy that you're all right."

"I'm so sorry," I said.

"Oh, Honey. *We're* sorry. We're so sorry for how selfish we've been," my mother said.

I saw that she was wearing her wedding ring. She had taken it off months prior, after a particularly heated argument with my father. I couldn't imagine why she would be wearing it again now.

"Things are going to change from now on, Shelton. We're going to rebuild and become a family again," my father said with a sniffle. He began to cry again and then pulled me into his arms and hugged me hard.

"But ... aren't you guys getting divorced?" I asked, my wavering voice muffled by my father's shoulder.

"Oh, Shelton, I wish we would have told you sooner," my mother said.

"Told me what?" I asked.

"We're not getting divorced," she said. "We were going to tell you that night ... the day you left. We had decided to give things another shot, honey."

I listened in disbelief. *Am I really hearing this?* I asked myself.

"Your mother and I realized how much we still love each other. We want to make it work," my father said.

"And we love *you*, Shelton. We love you so much," my mother said. She absently wiped a tear rolling down her cheek. "We know things have been hard on you since ... since John died. We really do. Your father and I have been very, very selfish. We were so wrapped up in ourselves and that was wrong. It almost cost us our marriage, and then it almost cost us our child. We are so, so sorry, honey."

"But you left a note," I said. "You said you guys wanted to talk to me about something. You were always talking about divorce. I just figured."

"I'm so sorry, honey. I wish you would have just waited," she said. "We wanted to talk to you about being a family again. I wish I would have said that more clearly in the note. We just wanted to tell you to your face. Together."

My mother's words felt heavy, and they brought fresh tears to my eyes. I told them that I loved them and apologized again for putting them through all of this. My father told me that it was their fault and that I had nothing to be sorry for. He said that they would never let something like this happen again and that they were just happy to have their son back.

I walked out of the police station with them, trying to process everything. I was grateful that they hadn't yet asked me about the things that had happened. That would come later during our trip home, I was sure. The Mississippi police had already told them the horrible parts of the story anyway. For now, I wanted to appreciate the good stuff.

Outside, my mother smothered me with kisses, and I loved every minute of it. Despite all the terrible things that had happened, I was still able to find happiness in those moments. My parents loved me, and they were staying together. We were going to be a *family* again.

And we were going *home*.

* * *

Even though I felt like there was so much to say, we didn't talk much during the taxi ride to the airport. We just kept looking at each other and smiling, reassuring ourselves that we weren't dreaming. My mother did say she was going to make my favorite meal for me when we got home. I looked forward to that, having eaten nothing but Mulligan stew for a month.

As we waited to board the plane, my father turned toward me with a curious expression. "By the way, we understand about why you left. Because of us," he said. "But in the note *you* left, you said that something happened to Richie that we would see in the news. What did you mean by that?"

"What?" I asked. I was utterly confused at that point. Even if it hadn't been on the news, talk of Jim's murder would have surely spread around Overture. "How can you not know?"

"Not know *what*, Shelton?"

"About Richie killing Jim! How can you not know about that? Everyone must be talking about it back home, right?"

My parents looked at each other, bewildered. "Son, Jim's not dead. What are you talking about?"

I searched my father's eyes to see if he was playing some cruel joke on me, but he was completely serious.

"What do you mean he's not dead?" I said. "Richie told me all about it."

"Shelton, I was putting up missing child flyers again just the other night, and I saw him," my mother explained. "He was stumbling out of that bar on Blaine Street. He looked pretty beat up, but he was very much alive."

I looked at them in astonishment. *How is this possible?* I thought. In my mind, I sorted through Richie's account of the day he had fought with Jim. He had said he killed him by accidentally pushing him down the stairs and that his stepfather hadn't moved after the fall. He had said Jim was dead. I recalled asking him that day if he had checked Jim's pulse, and he had said no. *So Jim must have survived the fall. That means—*

What it meant was that we had never needed to run away.

I was overcome with a plethora of emotions. I was already devastated over the death of Richie, but it was even harder now knowing that it was all for nothing. Jim was alive, and my parents weren't getting a divorce. I blamed myself for not being smart enough to figure out that Jim could have survived. I should have told Richie to drive back there and check his pulse that day. We would have known then that Jim wasn't dead, and we could have figured things out from there. Maybe I could have gotten Richie to stay at my house while we called the police on Jim.

On top of that, once we got to Train Town, I never heeded any of Richie's warnings about Navy Neal. He *knew* there was something up with that bastard, but I wouldn't listen. We would have left there and made it to Mexico if I hadn't been so intent on staying. That was *twice* that I could have made a decision to avoid Richie dying.

I couldn't help but feel that I was partially responsible for his death.

* * *

Back in Overture, my parents received a phone call from Mississippi informing them that the autopsy of Dustin James had revealed the cause of death as tuberculosis. They indicated that because I had been in close contact with the deceased and my parents had been in close contact with me, we would all need to be tested and treated.

At the hospital, my parents tested negative, but I tested positive. The doctors prescribed me a two-month treatment of Isoniazid, Rifampicin, and Pyrazinamide, followed by a four-month treatment of just the Isoniazid and Rifampicin. It was a long six months of remembering to take pills, doctor follow-ups, and monitoring, but staying healthy and alive was all worth the struggle.

I asked my parents to inquire with the Mississippi police about the well-being of the hoboes who had been arrested and to find out whether or not they had contracted tuberculosis, but we never received a response.

While I was lying in bed at night, I often found myself wondering if all of them were okay. The ones who had been arrested were most likely given treatment, even if it was just to protect the correctional officers, but Fat Neck Charlie and Beef Wellington were out there somewhere. I had the horrible idea that they would someday suffer the same fate as Dusty, never going to the hospital for fear of the black bottle.

Chapter 14
CIGARETTES IN A CEMETERY

October 2008

I parked my Volvo in the lot at the Hickory Hill Cemetery and looked at the gate. Before I had moved to Cleveland with my parents in 1992, I had come here every day to visit my friend. My parents had decided on Cleveland, because that has been where my grandparents had lived. We wanted to start a new life together in a new place so we could try to forget. Forgetting may have been easy for my parents, but it was impossible for me.

Seventeen years ago today, I thought with a chill. *It's the anniversary of Richie's death.*

After Richie had died, his mother, Bianca, had arranged for his body to be shipped to Overture for his eternal rest. At the funeral, I saw evidence of Jim's handiwork firsthand. Bianca's arm was in a sling, and she walked with a pronounced limp. The night that Richie and I had left, Jim had beaten her pretty badly. He stood quietly beside her during the services, bowing his head and feigning grief. I wanted to kill him then.

As Richie was being lowered into the ground, I took Bianca aside and shared Richie's deep regret that he hadn't told her that he loved her the last night he had seen her. She wept convulsively when she heard this and squeezed my hand so hard that I thought the bones would break. From the corner of my eye, I saw Jim glaring at us suspiciously.

Bianca finally came to her senses, though, only after she had been forced to prematurely say good-bye to her fourteen-year-old son forever. That night, she tried to leave Jim. She had planned to stay with her friend until Jim could get his stuff out of her house. Apparently, Jim couldn't handle it, and he put her in the hospital with a serious injury.

Days later, she revealed the events of that night to an eager reporter at the hospital. The story ended up on the front page of the *Overture Gazette*, winning out over the usual bake sales and town meeting results. In the interview, she conveyed how she had boldly told Jim that he was responsible for her son's death and began packing her things. He snapped and smashed a beer bottle over her head. But even that hadn't been enough for him.

He commenced beating her to within an inch of her life. Then, he dragged her down the stairs and threw her up against the kitchen counter with enough force to make a horrible snapping noise in her back. She collapsed to the floor, screaming in pain. In his rage, he didn't notice—or didn't care—and continued kicking her while she lay on the floor.

Luckily, a former marine had been walking his dog by their house. He had overheard the screams and kicked the front door in. When he saw the situation, he subdued Jim and called the police. Bianca was then rushed to the hospital with a severe spinal injury, and despite the medical attempts to prevent the worst, she had become a paraplegic.

Jim was initially charged with first-degree assault and resisting arrest, but once the details of Richie's abuse were reported, another count of first-degree assault and aggravated felonious sexual assault were added. It was also discovered that he had an outstanding arrest warrant for simple assault down in Nashua. The judge denied bail at his arraignment. In the eight months leading up to the trial, Jim spent his nights and days pacing around a jail cell while Bianca stayed in a hospital, learning how to cope as a paraplegic.

My parents didn't want me to testify, but I convinced them to let me. I wanted to see that bastard dead, but if that wasn't possible, I would at least see him in jail for as long as possible. It was the least I could do for my best friend.

In the courtroom, I testified on Richie's behalf, telling the jury everything that Richie had divulged to me. I also told them everything that had happened after we had ran away and that I believed Richie would still be alive today if it hadn't been for the actions of Jim Kemp. As I spoke, I looked Jim in the eyes several times. I could see that he was seething and that he was probably fantasizing about my violent death, but I held his gaze intently. I would not let him intimidate me. Richie may have died, but his strength and courage lived on in me.

I would never again be afraid of someone else.

Understandably, Bianca did not have the same amount of courage. She shook uncontrollably on the witness stand, and her eyes remained only on her lawyer and the judge. But it was still brave of her to testify, to finally step forward and speak up. I was happy that she had, but I still couldn't completely forgive her for not coming forward sooner. Richie might still have been alive if she had.

Her testimony was heart-wrenching, though. The women on the jury cried almost as much as she did. She told the court about the terrible things Jim had done to her; how he would sometimes beat her into unconsciousness, and how she suffered unspeakable sexual abuse by him. She also revealed that he had gotten her pregnant, and when he had found out about it, he had kicked her repeatedly in the stomach, causing a painful miscarriage. All the while, her wheelchair glimmered in the sunlight pouring in from the courtroom windows, emphasizing her affirmation of Jim's violence.

At one point during her testimony, Jim erupted in fury. He stood up and yelled at Bianca, calling her a lying bitch and a slut and a whore. The jury watched in sympathy as Bianca whimpered and trembled on the stand. He was then subdued by the surrounding officers and guarded for the remainder of the trial. The disruption only added to the case against him.

When asked about Richie, she attested that she had witnessed several of the severe beatings he had endured at the hands of Jim but that she had never known about the sexual abuse. On cross-examination, Jim's defense attorney tried to mitigate her testimony by smugly asking her, "If you witnessed these *alleged* beatings, then why didn't you, as a *responsible* mother, do anything about it or at least call the police?"

When she answered that she had been afraid for her and her son's lives, the lawyer couldn't get back to his seat quickly enough. He had made the classic courtroom blunder of asking a question that he hadn't known the answer to, and his client had paid for it.

When all was said and done, Jim received three consecutive sentences, which equaled over fifty years in the New Hampshire State Prison over in Concord. The injuries he had received from Richie had since healed, but I later heard that he sustained much worse wounds from his fellow inmates during the first few weeks he was in jail. Part of me hoped that Richie could rest in peace knowing that.

* * *

I got out of the car and walked through the cemetery gates. The autumn wind cooled my skin as I strode through the rows of tombstones to Richie's grave. When I finally got to his resting place, I saw that it had been slightly neglected. The grass was overgrown on the sides of his marker, obstructing part of his name, and the built-in vase was empty. No one was around to take care of his grave anymore.

Bianca had died two years ago from heart failure. Jim's beatings had damaged her body beyond repair, and in her final days, she had become bedridden. When the end had finally come, her heart had just stopped. She had been clutching a picture of her dead son. The newspapers had brazenly reported that she had died from a broken heart.

I brushed the dust off of Richie's grave marker and pried some of the grass away from the sides. A chill sliced through me as I read the bronze letters of my old friend's epitaph:

RICHARD WAYNE GALLO
JULY 30, 1977 ~ OCT. 18, 1991
A BOY IN DEATH
BUT HIS WAS A MAN'S COURAGE

After Jim was incarcerated, Bianca purchased a new grave marker, changing Richie's surname back to his birth name of Gallo. That way, he could rest in peace without any ties to Jim Kemp. I thought that was a nice touch. A single tear cruised down my face. I was surprised, because I hadn't thought I would cry today.

"Well, Richie," I said to his grave. "I'm here."

A flock of birds scattered from a nearby tree and flew somewhere unseen, giving me another chill.

"I came for our thirty-year caucus. It's not under the circumstances that we had hoped for, but I suppose it will have to do. I remember that night, sitting in the IROC-Z in that West Virginia parking lot. That's when we talked about it. You said that we would get together and smoke a cigarette for old time's sake. Well, like I said, here I am."

I felt a lump forming in my throat, and my eyes filled with tears. I glanced up at the sky to compose myself. Hissing air out from between my lips, I fumbled around in my pocket for my cigarette pack and lighter. As I took a cigarette out and put it between my lips, I noticed that there was only one more left in my pack. An idea came to me.

Fuck it, I thought. *He would get a kick out of this.*

I took the other cigarette out and lit them both. With my index finger, I bore a small hole in the ground where I thought Richie's head would have been and stuck the butt end of the second cigarette in it. Then I sat on the ground next to him in silence and started smoking my cigarette. I watched as the smoke curled from the slowly burning cigarette sticking out of the ground and wafted into the air and then disappeared. Every now and then, a small breeze would blow, making the lit end of the cigarette glow brighter, which gave the appearance that Richie was actually taking puffs off it.

That made me smile.

When I finished my cigarette, I flicked it away and took Tiffany's note from my pocket. The creases were marked with dirt, and the paper crackled as I opened it. I had saved it all these years and had decided that because I was letting go of my past today, I would also get rid of her note. I read it one last time, though. "Just for shits and giggles," as Richie would have said.

It would have been great to say that Tiffany and I lived happily ever after when I came back to Overture, but that just didn't happen. Things had changed when I had gotten back to school two weeks after I had returned from Mississippi. People, including Tiffany, didn't talk to me much at first. All of the other students and even the teachers treated me as if I had returned from some war in another country, as if I might have snapped and killed someone if they had said the wrong thing to me. I hadn't helped matters, either. I hadn't been very talkative when I had returned to school. I had withdrawn, keeping mostly to myself, because I was still overcome with grief.

I was an outcast at Overture High School once again.

After a while, as I healed, I became more social, and so did they; however, Tiffany had found someone else by that time, a football player named Billy Greer. When my parents and I moved to Cleveland, Tiffany and Billy were still together. I heard that they had married after high school and now had children. I thought about her from time to time but not in a romantic way. I mostly just thought about the way she had looked when she had come out of the crowd the day of Richie's fight with Wuzzy. She had been so beautiful back then.

Wuzzy had also changed. I had been afraid that he would terrorize me on my first day back, but he never said a word to me. He had stopped hitting other students and had begun hitting the books. He applied himself to his schoolwork and wasn't held back any longer. He had finally graduated, with honors even, and he had eventually enrolled in law school.

When the cigarette in the ground finally burned out, I removed it and threw it in a nearby trash can, along with Tiffany's note. As

I raised my arms above my head and stretched, I gazed at the sky above and wondered if Richie was up there looking down on me.

"Well, I guess that's it," I said, looking at his grave again. "I hope that you are resting in peace, my friend. I came here mostly because I've been seeing you in my dreams a lot. I was hoping that I could finally get on with my life, if that's okay. I just—"

Suddenly, I got choked up. I pressed my finger and thumb on the sides of my nose. Saying what I needed to say was a little harder than I had thought it would be. *Could he hear me from somewhere up there?* I wondered. *And if so, how would he feel about me telling him that I wanted to forget about him?* No, that wasn't right. Not forget. Just move on.

I took a deep breath and then continued, "Your last words to me were 'don't ever forget me.' I guess what I want to tell you is that I have never forgotten you and I never will, but I have to move on, Richie. I hope that you understand. I'm pretty sure you do. I'm sure it's just me being stupid and feeling guilty. That's something I can't change. You're lying down there, and I'm up here, going on with life. It's not fair. You deserved more of a chance in life."

I cleared my throat and then started again, "But I learned a lot from you, Richie. You told me one time that I'm a good person and that good things should happen to me. I hope you're right."

I put my hands in my pockets and fidgeted, patting some grass down with my foot.

"I, uh … I met a woman earlier this year. Her name is Meghan. She is very beautiful, and she's smart as a whip. She is perfect to me, and I want to make things work with her. I just need to shed all of this negativity and guilt I've been carrying around for years. Like I said, it's time for me to move on."

An airplane flew overhead, leaving a white trail in its wake. After the noise died down, I took a deep breath and continued, "You know, right before you died, you told me that it was the last stop on the train of consequences. Well, that wasn't the last stop for me, Richie. I've been on that train, dealing with the consequences ever since that day. The pain and guilt has never gone away, and it has affected everything I do. But it ends today. I'm decommissioning the train for good, Richie.

"So, I just wanted to come here to tell you that even though I've started a new life and even though I might not think about you every day, I will always remember you. And even though there is a different last name from mine on your gravestone, you are still my brother. And you always will be. Good-bye, Richie."

I bowed my head in silence for a minute and then walked out of the cemetery, knowing that I would finally get a good night's sleep, knowing that Richie was somewhere up there with Dusty and John, and they are all running free.

Epilogue
CLEVELAND BOUND

When I returned to Cleveland, I felt refreshed. I told my therapist all about my trip—that I had stopped having the recurring dreams and that I even quit smoking, the cigarette at Richie's grave being my last. She told me that saying good-bye to Richie and honoring the thirty-year caucus had been the ideal way for me to attain the closure I had needed so much. She also explained that seeing how my childhood town of Overture had changed and how *it* had moved on was just the assurance that I had needed in order to realize that it was okay to move on with my own life. She then told me that I might now be able to finally commit to my relationship with my girlfriend, Meghan, after I had released all of those pent up emotions and fears. This commitment, my therapist said, was also something that she could help me with if I continued my visits with her. For a hefty fee, of course.

One thing hadn't changed: I still thought my therapist was full of shit.

Nevertheless, I heeded her advice again and worked things out with my Meghan. I finally had a long talk with her about the things that had happened to me. She listened patiently and never once judged me. She even cried when I told her about Richie's tragic ending. When I finished telling her my tale, she kissed me on the forehead and told me that she was happy I had opened up to her and that she loved me.

We then worked together to shed my fears of intimacy and abandonment. I found myself finally willing to commit and open up to her so much that I asked her to marry me. She answered yes and embraced me with tears in her eyes. I cried, too, and realized that they were my first truly *happy* tears.

After a beautiful wedding and honeymoon, we bought ourselves a modest house down the street from my parents, who incidentally were still together and still happy, and created an ideal home. It was the perfect shelter from the hardness of the world—the place where she and I could be ourselves and love each other unconditionally, without restraint.

The following year, on April 17th, we had a premature but healthy baby boy together. It was truly the happiest day of my life. When he was born and the doctor handed him to me, I proudly held him in my arms. He opened his tiny blue eyes and looked right into mine. I swore to him and to myself right then and there that I would do everything in my power to be the best possible father that I could and that I would protect him with everything I had—this tiny fragile life that we created.

We named him Richard John Cole.

LaVergne, TN USA
22 December 2010
209831LV00004B/129/P